Helen W. Pierson

The Bible Story
in easy words for children

ISBN/EAN: 9783337392727

Printed in Europe, USA, Canada, Australia, Japan

Cover: Foto ©Andreas Hilbeck / pixelio.de

More available books at **www.hansebooks.com**

Helen W. Pierson

The Bible Story

in easy words for children

THE BIBLE STORY.

IN EASY WORDS FOR CHILDREN.

BUILDING THE TOWER OF BABEL.

BY

MRS. HELEN W. PIERSON,

AUTHOR OF "HISTORY OF UNITED STATES," "HISTORY OF ENGLAND," ETC., ETC., ETC., IN WORDS OF
ONE SYLLABLE.

NEW YORK:

MCLOUGHLIN BROTHERS, PUBLISHERS.

PREFACE.

It has not been thought advisable, in this story of the Bible, to adhere to words of one syllable quite so strictly as has been done in some other works. Simple and easy words have been used which a child can read, but in order to convey exact statements these words are sometimes of two syllables.

The liberties taken with other histories cannot be taken with the Bible. In places where the exact words could be used, they have been used. Where they were difficult, they have been put in a simpler form, but it is hoped that the dignity and beauty of the words of Holy Writ have not been sacrificed.

H. W. P.

CONTENTS.

CHAPTER I.

HOW GOD MADE THE WORLD.

THERE was a time a great while a-go when there was no world, or sun, or moon and stars. All was dark.

Then God said, "Let there be light!" and there was light.

He called the time when it was light, Day; and the time when it was dark, Night.

God made these on the first day.

The next day He made the sky and called it Heav-en.

On the third day He made the Sea and the dry land. He called the dry land Earth, and He made the grass to grow on it and the flow-ers to bloom and trees to bear fruit. And each tree and flow-er bore seed that could be plant-ed so as to bring forth more of its kind.

On the fourth day God made a great light which He set in the sky. He called it the Sun and it gives us light by day. He made the Moon and stars to shine at night.

On the fifth day God made all the fish that swim in the sea and the birds that fly in the air.

On the sixth day God made beasts of all the kinds that are on the earth, and all things that creep on the earth.

And on this day, too, God made man.

He made him king of all things that lived on the earth, and gave him the fruit of the land for his food.

"THEN GOD SAID, 'LET THERE BE LIGHT'"

Then God rest-ed from His work on the sev-enth day, so it has been kept as a day of rest from that time.

Man was made from the dust of the ground. God breathed in-to it the breath of life—and man lived. A gar-den was his home where all sorts of fruits grew that were good to eat. There was a stream that flowed through the place and kept all green.

God called the man's name Ad-am, and He told him that he could eat the fruit of all the trees in the gar-den of E-den but one tree. That was called the tree of "The Know-ledge of Good and E-vil. God said to Ad-am, "In the day thou eat-est of that fruit thou shalt sure-ly die."

Then God saw that it was not good for the man to live a-lone and He made Ad-am fall in a deep sleep.

While he slept God took a rib from his side and made a wo-man. He gave her to Ad-am for his wife, and her name was called Eve.

And God sent all the beasts and the birds to Ad-am to be named by him.

Now the e-vil one wished to tempt Eve to sin. So he took the form of a ser-pent, or snake.

He said to Eve, "Yea! hath God said ye shall not eat of all the fruit of the gar-den?"

THE SIN OF AD-AM AND EVE.

Eve said that they might eat of all the fruit but from one tree, and if they ate of that they would die.

But Sa-tan said, "Ye shall not die, but ye will be wise as gods."

So Eve looked at the tree and saw that the fruit was fair and good. So she took some of it and ate it and gave some to Ad-am.

Then they heard the voice of God, and they were a-fraid and hid in the trees. But God said, "Ad-am where art thou?"

And Ad-am came out and said, "I heard thee but I was a-fraid and hid."

Then God said, "Hast thou eat-en of the fruit of that tree I for-bade thee to eat?"

And Ad-am said, "The wo-man gave it to me and I did eat."

Then God said to Eve, "What is this that thou hast done?"

And Eve said, "The ser-pent tempt-ed me and I did eat."

And God was wroth with them, and said that the ser-pent should be cursed. It would have to crawl in the dust all the days of its life. He drove Ad-am and Eve out of the gar-den, and set an-gels to keep watch with swords of fire that turned each way so that they could not go back.

God told Eve that she should have much pain and sor-row in her life, and to Ad-am He said that the ground would not bear fruit a-ny more for him un-less he worked hard, and that when he died his bod-y would go back to dust like the dust out of which the Lord had made him.

So the two went out in-to the world. God gave them coats made out of the skins of an-i-mals to keep them from the cold.

AD-AM AND EVE DRIV-EN FROM THE GAR-DEN.

They had two sons born to them. The eld-est was named Cain and the oth-er A-bel.

Cain tilled the ground and raised fruit, but A-bel kept sheep.

And A-bel loved God and sought to give the best of his flock to him, but Cain's heart was hard, and though

he brought the fruit of his land he did not do it with love.
God said to Cain that if he did right he would be pleased
with him, but if he would not the fault was his own.

So Cain grew to hate A-bel, and one day when they
were out in the field he killed him, and his blood stained
the ground.

When God called to Cain " Where is A-bel?" Cain said
"I know not. Am I my broth-er's keep-er?"

Then God said, " What hast thou done ? The voice of
thy broth-er's blood cri-eth to me from the ground!"

And God told Cain that for this sin he should have no
home on the earth, no place where he could stay long, but
he must move on and on till he died.

THE FRUITS OF SIN.

CAIN AND A-BEL OF-FER-ING THEIR GIFTS TO GOD.

Then Cain said, "That is more than I can bear. The hand of all men will be a-gainst me, and they will kill me." But God set a mark on his fore-head so that all would know who he was and his life should be safe.

Ad-am and Eve lived a long time and they had more chil-dren. In those days men lived much long-er than they do now.

Ad-am lived nine hun-dred and thir-ty years. Then his bod-y went to dust a-gain—as God had said.

The name of one of the men who lived in those days was E-noch. It is told of him that he walked with God. This means that the thought of God's love for him was in his heart all the time. E-noch did not die like all oth-er men. God took him right up to Heav-en a-live. E-noch had a son named Me-thu-se-lah who was the old-est man that ev-er lived. When he died he was nine hun-dred and six-ty-nine years old.

CHAPTER II.

A-BOUT THE ARK.

In time the men in the world grew so full of sin that God said He would sweep them from the face of the earth.

But there was a good man named No-ah that God loved. So He told him of the great flood He meant to send to wash the world clean once more.

He want-ed to save No-ah so He told him to build an ark—a sort of house that could float on the wa-ter. He said that No-ah might save his own chil-dren, and take two of all kinds of beasts and birds and in-sects in-to the ark. All that were left would be drowned.

It took a long time to build the ark, for it was three stories high and of a great size. When it was done No-ah went in with his wife and three sons and their wives. All the beasts and birds and in-sects were tak-en in, two by two, and shut in safe.

Then it be-gan to rain, and did not stop for for-ty days and nights. All the land was covered, and at last there was not a green thing to be seen. Ev-er-y liv-ing thing on the face of the earth was drowned.

BUILD-ING THE ARK.

But No-ah and all those in the ark were safe and at last the wa-ter be-gan to leave the earth.

The tops of mount-ains could be seen and the ark rest-ed on one called Ar-a-rat. No-ah and those with him had lived in the ark five months and they had to stay two months more. Then No-ah let a ra-ven go out, but it did not come back.

The next bird he sent was a dove, but she found no place to rest and so she came back to him. He wait-ed a week and sent her out once more. This time she came

back with an ol-ive leaf in her bill. Then No-ah knew
that the wa-ters must have gone down and that the ground
would soon be dry. He wait-ed one week more and sent
out the dove. She did not come back, so he was sure she
had found a dry place and that it was safe for all to go
out of the ark. When they were all on dry ground No-ah
built an al-tar to God, and of-fered up an-i-mals and birds
on it, to show his thanks to the Lord who had saved them
from the great flood.

And God loved No-ah and told him he might be mas-

AFT-ER THE FLOOD.

ter of all liv-ing things and kill what was good for food. He said that He would send no more floods, and as a pledge of this He set a sign in the sky that would come aft-er a rain. It is what is called a rain-bow.

No-ah lived a long time aft-er the flood. He was nine hun-dred and fif-ty years old when he died.

No-ah's sons had chil-dren and these in turn grew up and had sons and daugh-ters so that the world grew full of peo-ple in time. They sinned and did not fear God. They all spoke one lan-guage in those days, and they went to work to build a high tow-er on a plain called Shi-nar. They thought per-haps if a new flood came they could be safe from God's wrath on it.

But when God saw it He was wroth and He made them all at once speak in strange tongues, so they could not go on. No one knew what the oth-er meant and the work had to be stopped. The tow-er they tried to build was called from that day the tow-er of Ba-bel.

Long years aft-er there lived a man in the land of Ur called A-bram. God told him to leave his home, and though he did not know where he was to go, he took his wife and his broth-er's son, Lot, and set out for the land where God was to lead him. God took care of him on the way and gave him the land called Ca-naan to be his and his chil-dren's. He had herds of sheep and cows, and was a rich man. But they did not live in hous-es in those days. They put up tents and let the sheep and cows graze on the grass in one place till it was all gone and then they moved on.

They had herds-men to take care of the flocks, and these men did not live in peace, so A-bram said to Lot that he could choose what part of the land he would like to live in and he would go some-where else.

So Lot chose a plain through which the Jor-dan flowed. There was a cit-y there named Sod-om which was full of bad men. Lot thought he could still serve God and live with these bad men, and grow more rich.

The Lord told A-bram that the land as far as he could see should be his own.

A-bram built three al-tars to the Lord to show his love for Him.

It came to pass that four kings who ruled in the parts near Sod-om, went to war with that cit-y, and took it and all that was in it. Lot was seized with the rest and held as a slave. When A-bram heard this he called his men and came up to the four kings and their troops and fought them. God helped him to win the fight, and Lot and all the rest were set free, and all the gold and gems fell in-to A-bram's hands. He did not keep it for him-self though, but gave it all to those who had helped him in the fight.

A-bram had no child and God said He would give him a son. He told A-bram to look up at the stars and see if he could count them, and He said his chil-dren's chil-dren should be like those stars, they would be so ma-ny. Some of them would be kings. And He called his name A-bra-ham, which means "Fa-ther of ma-ny peo-ple."

A-bra-ham was sit-ting in his tent door one day, when

he saw three men near him. He bowed down to them, as was the way in those days, and asked them to rest, and brought wa-ter to wash their feet. There were no shoes in those days, but peo-ple wore things like the soles of our shoes strapped to their feet. So it was the cus-tom to give the guest a chance to bathe his feet.

A-bra-ham brought them bread too, and told Sa-rah his wife to bake some cakes. Then he took a calf and had it killed, and set all be-fore the men and they ate. When they were done they walked on to Sod-om and A-bra-ham went with them.

LOT FLIES FROM SOD-OM.

But we are told that these were not mere men. Two were an-gels, and one was the Lord, who took the form of man.

He talked with A-bra-ham and told him that He meant to burn the cit-ies of Sod-om and Go-mor-rah for the sin in them. Now Lot lived in Sod-om and A-bra-ham feared that he would lose his life. So he spoke to the Lord and said that it might be there were good men in the place. The Lord said if there were ten good men in it He would not burn it.

Lot sat at the gate of Sod-om that night, and the two an-gels in the form of men came to him and told him that if he had sons and daugh-ters he must take them and fly, for the Lord meant to burn Sod-om. But Lot's sons would not hear him and he had to leave them. The an-gels told him he must go at once, and make great haste. So Lot went with his wife and two daugh-ters. But as they went forth Lot's wife looked back on Sod-om, which she had been told not to do, and so she died, and was turned in-to a pil-lar of salt.

When A-bra-ham looked in the morn-ing he saw a great smoke where the two cit-ies had been, and he knew that there had not been found ten good men in Sod-om.

God gave to A-bra-ham and his wife a son, and they called his name I-saac. When he had grown a large boy they made a feast for him one day. One of his wife, Sa-rah's, maids whose name was Ha-gar had a son too, called Ish-ma-el. This boy mocked at I-saac, and Sa-rah said he must go a-way. A-bra-ham called Ha-gar and

HA-GAR GOES FORTH WITH HER SON.

told her and gave her some bread and a bot-tle of wa-ter. The bot-tles then were made of skins of beasts.

Ha-gar went forth with her boy. When all the wa-ter was gone, she saw her child grow weak and she thought he would die. She laid him in the shade and went a-way to weep. She could not bear to see her boy die.

The an-gel of God heard her and told her not to fear, but to take up Ish-ma-el and hold him in her arms. Then she saw all at once a well near her, and she gave the child a drink, and he grew well and strong.

CHAPTER III.

ONE day God called A-bra-ham, and he said, "Here am I."

And God said, "Take now thy son, thine on-ly son, I-saac, whom thou lov-est, and get thee to the land of Mar-ah, and of-fer him up to me on one of the moun-tains I will tell thee of."

Did not that seem a hard thing that A-bra-ham was asked to do — to kill his own son and lay him on an al-tar, and put wood un-der it and set it on fire, and burn him as he had done with the young lambs he of-fered to God? But he did not think that God would harm him. He had faith in Him. He knew He had done him good all the days of his life. So he rose up in the morn-ing and took two men with the wood all cut to lay on the al-tar. He called his son I-saac and they set out for the place. When it was in sight, he left the two men and went on with his son. The boy took the wood and A-bra-ham had the fire and a knife in his hand.

I-saac did not know what was to be done. He asked, "Fa-ther, you have the fire and the wood, but where is the lamb?"

A-bra-ham said, "My son, God will find a lamb." So they came to the place God had told him of, and A-bra-ham built the al-tar and put the wood on it. Then he bound his son and laid him on the wood and stretched out his hand for the knife.

But just then the an-gel of the Lord called to him and he said, " Here am I."

And the an-gel said, " Lay not thine hand up-on the lad, for now I know that thou dost fear God, since thou hast not kept back thy son, thine on-ly son."

" AND THE AN-GEL SAID, ' LAY NOT THINE HAND UP-ON THE LAD.' "

And A-bra-ham saw a ram that was caught fast in the bush-es by his horns, and he took it and put it on the al-tar and of-fered it up in the place of his son.

And God was pleased with him, and said that in his seed all the na-tions of the earth should be blessed. By this he meant that Christ should be born of the tribe of A-bra-ham, to save men from their sins.

Then Sa-rah, the wife of A-bra-ham, died, and he mourned for her, and asked for a place where she might be bur-ied. The pla-ces where the dead were bur-ied in those days were caves cut out of the rock. A great stone was placed at the door to shut it up. A man named E-phron came and said he would give his cave to A-bra-ham. But A-bra-ham bought the field and cave from him and there he bur-ied Sa-rah.

He was an old man then and his son I-saac was grown. He did not wish him to take a wife who did not love the true God, but bowed down to gods of wood and stone. So he sent a man to his own land to bring back a wife for his son.

The man, who had the care of A-bra-ham's herds, took ten cam-els and some rich gifts and set out for the land to which he had been sent. When he got to a well near a town in that land, he made the cam-els kneel down so that he could take off their loads and let them rest.

The wo-men of the place used to come to that well to draw wa-ter, and the man prayed to God to help him choose the right one to be I-saac's wife. He thought he would ask for a drink of wa-ter to see which one would be the most kind. While he prayed, a young girl named Re-bek-ah came with a pitch-er and filled it at the well. Then the ser-vant ran and met her and said, "Give me, I pray, a drink out of thy pitch-er." She said, "Drink and I will draw wa-ter for thy cam-els too."

So she ran to the well and drew wa-ter for them. Then the man took ear-rings of gold and brace-lets and gave them to Re-bek-ah. He asked her of her home and if there was room there for him to stay with his men. She said that her fa-ther's name was Be-thu-el and that he could stay at their house. Then the man knew she was kin to A-bra-ham.

Re-bek-ah ran home and told of all these things. When her broth-er La-ban heard it he went out and found the man still at the well. He asked him to come to their house and the man did so. They gave him straw and food for his cam-els, and set out food for the men with him to eat. But the ser-vant of A-bra-ham would not eat till he told them why he had come in-to their land. He told them how God had blessed A-bra-ham and made him rich and great. He spoke of his son I-saac, and how he wished to find a wife for him who loved God, and how he had prayed to know the right one to choose. He then asked if they would let Re-bek-ah go home with him to be I-saac's wife. They said that if it was the will of God she might go. The ser-vant knelt down and thanked God. Then he brought out the gifts of gold and sil-ver and gave them to Re-bek-ah and her friends. When this was done they all ate and drank and they slept at La-ban's house that night.

At first Re-bek-ah's friends did not wish to part with her for a few days. But the man begged them to let her

go with him at once. She was called and she said, "I will
go."   So they set out and rode on the cam-els till they
came to the land of Ca-naan.

I-SAAC AND RE-BEK-AH.

The sun was just set-ting as they reached there. I-saac
had gone out in the field to walk and as he looked up he
saw the cam-els.   Re-bek-ah asked the ser-vant who the
man was that was com-ing to meet them.   He said it was
I-saac.   So Re-bek-ah got down off her cam-el and met
I-saac and he led her to the tent.   He took her for his
wife and loved her all the days of his life.

Then A-bra-ham died and was bur-ied in the cave

where his wife slept, and all his rich-es were left to his son, I-saac.

God gave I-saac and Re-bek-ah two sons. E-sau was the first born and Ja-cob was the young-er. In those days the first born had a right to more than all the rest. He had a right to twice as much of the wealth his fa-ther might leave when he died, and this was called his birth-right. .

E-sau was fond of the hunt, but Ja-cob stayed at home and tend-ed the flocks.

One day Ja-cob had made some food called pot-tage. E-sau came in ver-y faint and hun-gry and asked for some. Ja-cob told him he would give him some if he would sell him his birth right. E-sau said, "I am at the point to die, so what good shall this birth right do me." So he sold it. This was wrong in E-sau, and it was a sin too for Ja-cob to take it from him.

CHAPTER IV.

JA-COB BLESSED BY I-SAAC.—LE-AH AND RA-CHEL.

THERE came a time when food was scarce in the land of Ca-naan, and I-saac moved to a new place called Ge-rar. There he sowed seed, and the Lord blessed the land so that it brought forth large crops for him, and he grew rich and great.

But the king of the land would not let him stay there.

So he took his wife and his herds and moved on and found
the wells his fa-ther had dug when he camped at that
place. And the Lord told I-saac not to fear, for He
would take care of him and bless him.

E-sau took for his wife a wo-man of Ca-naan who did
not pray to the true God, but bowed down to gods of
wood and stone. Now I-saac was an old man and he
thought his death was near. So he called E-sau one day
and told him to go out and kill a deer, and cook part
of it and bring it to him to eat. Then he said he would
bless him be-fore he died.

Now Re-bek-ah heard this and she loved Ja-cob the
most. So when E-sau had gone to the hunt, she made
haste and took two kids and cooked them. Then she told
Ja-cob to put on some of E-sau's clothes and take the food
to his fa-ther.

I-saac's sight was dim, so that he could not tell which
of his sons had brought him the food. Ja-cob said he
was E-sau, and so his fa-ther blessed him, and told him he
should be lord, and all should serve him and bow down
to him. When Ja-cob had gone, E-sau came in from the
hunt, and I-saac asked, "Who art thou?"

E-sau said, "I am thy son, thy first born, E-sau."

I-saac shook with fear, "Who is it that brought the food
to me that I have eat-en? I have blessed him, and he shall
be blessed."

And E-sau wept and cried, "Bless me too, my fa-ther."
And I-saac did bless him, but the best things had been
giv-en to Ja-cob and he could not take them from him.

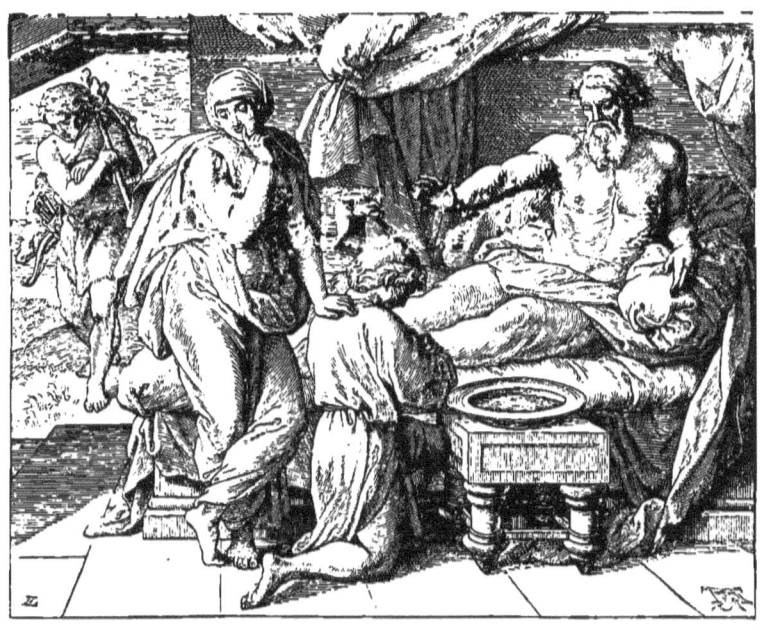

JA-COB IS BLESSED BY I-SAAC.

It was a great sin for Ja-cob to do this thing, and for
his moth-er to help him. E-sau hat-ed his broth-er for
this, and thought he would kill him as soon as his fa-ther
died. Re-bek-ah feared this, so she sent for Ja-cob and
told him to go to her old home, where he could find a wife.

So Ja-cob set out on the road, and when the sun was
set he stopped to rest. He lay down on the ground and
slept, and dreamed that he saw a lad-der that reached up
to Heav-en, and an-gels went up and down on it. The
Lord told him He would give him the land of Ca-naan,
and bring him back safe. When Ja-cob woke he gave

thanks to the Lord, and called that place Beth-el, which means, "The House of God."

And Ja-cob said that if the Lord would take care of him, he would serve Him all his life and give a tenth part of all he had to Him. By this he meant that he would use a tenth part of his wealth for the sick and poor, and to raise al-tars to God.

Then Ja-cob went on to the place where La-ban lived. He stopped at a well in a field where there were some shep-herds with their sheep. Ja-cob asked them if they knew a man named La-ban. They said they knew him

JA-COB'S DREAM.

well, and that his daugh-ter Ra-chel was com-ing just then with his sheep.

Ja-cob ran to the well and drew the wa-ter for Ra-chel's sheep, and spoke to her and told her who he was.

She made haste home and told her fa-ther, and he came out to meet Ja-cob. He took him to his home and beg-ged him to stay there. He said he would pay him if he would stay with him and take care of his flocks. Ja-cob told him he would work for him sev-en years if at the end of them he would give him Ra-chel for his wife. La-ban said he would and Ja-cob stayed and worked for sev-en years. He loved Ra-chel so much that the time did not seem long.

But when the end of the sev-en years came, La-ban did not keep his word. He said he would not give him Ra-chel un-less he worked for him sev-en years more; for it was the way in that land for the eld-est to mar-ry first. Now Le-ah, his first born, was not so fair as Ra-chel, but Ja-cob took her for his wife Then La-ban gave him Ra-chel, and he worked for him sev-en years more.

At the end of this time Ja-cob wished to go home, but La-ban told him the Lord had blessed him so much while he had been with him that he did not want him to go. He asked Ja-cob what he could give him to make him stay. Ja-cob told him if he would give him a share in the herds and flocks he would stay for a time.

Now Ja-cob's flock grew to be a great ma-ny and he was so rich that La-ban's sons did not like it. They said he had grown rich from their fa-ther's cat-tle. La-ban was

JA-COB AND RA-CHEL AT THE WELL.

changed too and was not kind, so God told Ja-cob to go
back to his own land. He said He would take care of
him and keep him safe.

So Ja-cob told his wives, and they said he must do as
the Lord bade him. He had cam-els brought and put his
wives and chil-dren on them, and he took his flocks and
herds and all that he owned and set out for Ca-naan.
La-ban did not know at first that he had gone, but some
one told him on the third day. So he rose up and took
some men with him to go and find Ja-cob. He was an-gry
but God spoke to him in a dream and told him he must
not harm Ja-cob.

He did not find him for sev-en days. When he met him and asked him why he had gone in that way, Ja-cob told him he feared he would keep Ra-chel and Le-ah if he knew. He told how long he had served in the heat and cold, and said that if God had not helped him, La-ban would not have paid him for the work.

Then La-ban said they would be friends, and they piled up a heap of stones in that place, which was to stay there al-ways to keep them in mind of what they had said. And Ja-cob built an al-tar there and he and La-ban prayed to God.

Then La-ban kissed his chil-dren and went back to his own home. That place was called Mount Gil-e-ad.

CHAPTER V.

JO-SEPH AND HIS BRETH-REN.

WHEN Ja-cob came near to the place where E-sau lived he sent word to him. He thought of his sin a-gainst E-sau when they were young, and he feared to meet his bro-ther.

The ser-vants came back and told him that E-sau was com-ing to meet him with four hun-dred men. Then Ja-cob was in great fear, for he thought E-sau meant to kill him.

He prayed to God to keep him safe. At night, an an-gel came and wrest-led with him till break of day, but

could not over-come him. And when morn came, the
an-gel said, "Let me go, for it is break of day." Ja-cob
said, "I will not let thee go till thou bless me." Then the
an-gel blessed him, and he saw him no more. This was a
sign from God to Ja-cob that as he was a match for an
an-gel, he need not fear men.

JA-COB WRES-TLING WITH THE AN-GEL.

He took some of his cat-tle and sent them as a gift to
E-sau. He set them in droves so that when E-sau met
them and asked whose they were, the man should say,
"They are Ja-cob's. It is a gift he has sent to my lord
E-sau." Each man who drove the cat-tle was to an-swer

in this way, so that E-sau might feel that Ja-cob had come as a friend.

All at once Ja-cob looked up and saw E-sau com-ing. Then he called his e-lev-en sons with Ra-chel and Le-ah to go with him and meet E-sau. But he went first.

When he met E-sau he bowed down to the ground sev-en times. Then E-sau ran to him and put his arms round his neck and kissed him and they both wept.

E-sau saw the wo-men and chil-dren, and asked, "Who are these?"

Ja-cob said, "These are my wives and the chil-dren

THE MEET-ING OF JA-COB AND E-SAU.

God has giv-en me." Then E-sau asked Ja-cob what he meant by all the cat-tle he had met on the way. Ja-cob said that they were a gift to him. But E-sau told him he was rich and did not need gifts. Still Ja-cob begged him to take them, and at last he did so.

Then E-sau said he would stay with Ja-cob and go on with him a lit-tle way. But Ja-cob told him he could not trav-el fast as the chil-dren were young and that it would be best for E-sau to go first and he would come on as he could.

Then E-sau wished to leave some of his men to help him, but Ja-cob did not need them.

When Ja-cob reached the land of Ca-naan, God told him to go to Beth-el and build an al-tar. Beth-el was the place where he had dreamed of the an-gels that went up and down the lad-der.

So Ja-cob told his wives of all the Lord had done for him, and they went with him to Beth-el and built the al-tar and praised God.

And God spoke to Ja-cob, and blessed him, and said, "Thy name shall not be called Ja-cob a-ny more but Is-ra-el shall be thy name."

Ja-cob set up a pil-lar in Beth-el to mark the place where God had talked with him.

Then they left Beth-el and came near a place called Beth-le-hem, where God gave Ja-cob a son who was named Ben-ja-min. But Ra-chel died there and was buried. Ja-cob set up a pil-lar to mark the grave, and it stood there for a long time.

Ja-cob found that his fa-ther still lived in He-bron. It had been ma-ny years since the day I-saac had blessed Ja-cob in the place of E-sau, yet God had kept him a-live till he saw his son once more. He died when he was a hun-dred and eigh-ty years old, and he was laid to rest in the same cave in which A-bra-ham and Sa-rah were buried.

E-sau took his wives and chil-dren and went to the land of E-dom.

Now Ja-cob lived in the land of Ca-naan that God gave to his fa-ther.

And he had twelve sons. The youn-gest was Ben-ja-min. Jo-seph was next to him, and Ja-cob loved him be-cause he was the son of his old age, and he made him a coat of ma-ny col-ors. When his broth-ers saw that their fa-ther loved him so much they hat-ed him. He had seen them do wrong and told his fa-ther and this made them hate him the more. Once Jo-seph had a strange dream, and he told his broth-ers. He said, "We were bind-ing sheaves in the field, and lo! my sheaf a-rose and stood up-right, and your sheaves bowed down to my sheaf."

Then his broth-ers were in a rage, and they said, "Shalt thou reign over us?" and they hat-ed him all the more for his dreams. Still when he dreamed once more he told them of it. He said, "I dreamed the sun and moon and e-lev-en stars bowed down to me."

Now there were e-lev-en of the broth-ers, and they thought Jo-seph meant them by the e-lev-en stars, and that the moon and sun were his fa-ther and moth-er. His fa-ther said, "Shall I and thy moth-er and thy breth-ren bow down to thee to the earth?"

Now Jo-seph's broth-ers went with their flocks to She-chem.

And Jo-seph's fa-ther said to him, "Go I pray thee and see if it be well with thy breth-ren, and well with the flocks, and bring me word."

Jo-seph could not find them at first till he met a man who told him they had gone on to Do-than.

The broth-ers saw him when he was far off and they made a plot to kill him.

They said, "See this dream-er com-eth. Come, now, let us slay him and cast him in a pit, and we will say some e-vil beast has eat-en him, and we shall see what will come of his dreams."

But Reu-ben said, "Let us not kill him but cast him in the pit and leave him there." Now Reu-ben meant to save the boy's life. So when Jo-seph reached the place, they seized him and stripped off the coat of ma-ny col-ors and cast him in the pit. It was a dry pit so the boy was not drowned.

Then they sat down to eat. They did not care for the boy's fright or pain. As they ate they saw some men ride near on cam-els. These were Ish-ma-el-ites and they came from Gil-e-ad with spice and balm and myrrh which they meant to sell in E-gypt.

Then Ju-dah said, "Why should we leave the lad in the pit when we can get gold for him.? Let us sell him to these men."

JO-SEPH SOLD BY HIS BRETH-REN.

So they sold Jo-seph for twen-ty pie-ces of sil-ver.

Now Reu-ben was not with them when they sold the boy, and when he came back and went to the pit to take him out, he found that he was gone.

Then Reu-ben was in great grief, and he rent his clothes and cried, " The child is not, and I, whith-er shall I go ?"

Then they took Jo-seph's coat and killed a goat and dipped the coat in the blood. And they showed the coat to their fa-ther and said, " This have we found. Know now if it be thy son's coat or no."

And he knew it and said, "It is my son's coat."
And he thought some wild beast had killed him.
And he rent his clothes and mourned for his son a long
time. The men in those days wore a long coat made of
lin-en. It was made fast at the waist with a belt. When
in great grief they rent or tore this coat, and put on a
coarse kind of robe made of a cloth called sack-cloth, to
show their sor-row—just as peo-ple now put on black
clothes when they mourn for the dead.

CHAPTER VI.

HOW JO-SEPH WAS MADE GREAT.

Now the Ish-ma-el-ites took the boy Jo-seph down to
E-gypt. The King of that land was Pha-raoh, but the
man who was at the head of all his house was named
Pot-i-phar. Pot-i-phar bought Jo-seph and took him in
his house to serve him. And the Lord blessed him so
that Pot-i-phar trust-ed him.

But Pot-i-phar's wife told what was not true of Jo-seph,
so that, through no fault of his own, he was thrown in
pris-on. The Lord still took care of him, and the keep-er
of the pris-on was his friend, and gave him charge of all
the rest of the men who were there. Then there were two
new men cast in the pris-on. They were the chief ba-ker
and the chief but-ler to the king.

Now each of these men dreamed a dream the same

night, and in the morn-ing they looked sad. Jo-seph asked
them, "Why look ye so?" and they told him their dreams.

The chief but-ler, whose task it was to serve the king
with wine, said, " I thought I saw a vine, and on the vine
were three branch-es. And while I looked there came
out buds that soon changed to bunch-es of grapes. And I
pressed out the grapes in Pha-raoh's wine cup, and gave
him the juice to drink." .

So God showed Jo-seph what this dream meant, and he
told the man. He said the three branch-es meant three
days, and that in three days he would leave the pris-on
and go back to his place. Then he asked the man to
speak a good word for him when he went to serve Pha-
raoh once more.

The chief ba-ker then told Jo-seph his dream. He
said he thought he had three bas-kets on his head. In
the top bas-ket were all kinds of cooked meats, and the
birds flew down and eat them. Jo-seph told him that the
three bas-kets meant three days. He said that in three
days he would be hung on a tree, and the birds would
come and eat his flesh. This came true. In three days
the king made a great feast on his birth day, and he sent
for the chief but-ler and let him serve the wine as he had
done. But he had the chief ba-ker hanged.

Now the chief but-ler did not think of Jo-seph or speak
of him to Pha-raoh when he got back to his place. So
Jo-seph was left in pris-on two years.

Then Pha-roah dreamed a dream. He thought he saw
a riv-er, and sev-en cows came up out of it. They were

fat and fine and they ate grass in a field. Then came up sev-en thin, poor cows, and they seemed to eat up the sev-en fat ones.

He slept and dreamed once more. He saw sev-en ears of corn that grew on one stalk. They were plump and good. Then he saw sev-en bad ears that were not fit to eat, and these ate up the sev-en good ones.

When it was day, he sent and called for all the wise men of the land; but they could not tell him what was meant by his dream.

Then the chief but-ler thought of Jo-seph. He said to the king that when he was in pris-on there was a young man who had told him and the ba-ker what their dreams meant, and what he said had come true.

So Pha-raoh sent and called Jo-seph. He made haste and came to the king. Pha-raoh told him he had dreamed a dream and no one could tell what was meant, and he had heard of him that he knew how to read dreams. Jo-seph said that it was not he, but God who would tell him what he want-ed to know. So the king told his two dreams.

Then Jo-seph said that the Lord had made known by these two dreams what he meant to do. The sev-en good cows, and the sev-en good ears of corn, meant sev-en good years in the land, when the crops would grow well. Then the sev-en bad cows and bad ears of corn meant sev-en years when food would be scarce in the land.

So Jo-seph said that Pha-raoh should look for a wise man, who would see that the corn was stored up in the

JO-SEPH IN-TER-PRET-ING DREAMS.

sev-en good years, that the peo-ple might not starve in the time when food should be scarce. Pha-raoh thought that Jo-seph was just the right man to do this and he gave him the place.

So Jo-seph was a great man in the land, for the king took a gold ring off his own hand and put it on him, and put a rich robe on him and a gold chain on his neck and made him ride next to him. And as he rode all cried, "Bow the knee!" So he ruled over all the land of E-gypt.

Jo-seph was thir-ty years old at this time, and the king gave him a wife named As-e-nath. He went through the

land and saw that the corn was stored so as to keep it
safe till the sev-en bad years should come.

God gave Jo-seph two sons, and their names were
Ma-nas-seh and E-phra-im.

Then the sev-en good years came to an end and the bad
years be-gan. In all lands food was scarce, but in E-gypt
there was bread. Jo-seph took corn from the store hous-es
and sold it to the peo-ple, and when this was known in
oth-er lands men were sent to buy food in E-gypt.

Now Jo-seph's broth-ers still lived with their fa-ther
in Ca-naan. They did not know what had be-come of
Jo-seph, and they thought he was dead. Bread was scarce
in their land, and they feared they would starve. They
did not know what to do.

But Ja-cob said, "I have heard there is corn in E-gypt
—go down there and buy some for us that we may live
and not die."

So ten of them left their home, but Ben-ja-min, the
youn-gest, stayed with his fa-ther.

Now Jo-seph ruled all the land of E-gypt. When men
came to buy corn they had to see him first. So his
broth-ers came and bowed down to him. Jo-seph knew
them; but they did not know him, for he had changed in
the years since they had sold him. They did not dream
that this great lord in his rich robes was the child they
had thrown in the pit.

Then Jo-seph spoke in a harsh way to them. "From
whence do ye come?" he asked. They said, "We are
come from the land of Ca-naan to buy food."

But Jo-seph said, "Ye are spies—ye have come to find out all a-bout the land."

They said, "Nay, my lord, we are true men, we are not spies."

Jo-seph did not want them to know him yet, so he seemed hard with them. They told him of their fa-ther, and Ben-ja-min, the one at home. One, they said, was not. By this they meant one was dead.

Jo-seph knew they spoke of him.

Jo-seph said that one of them must go back and bring Ben-ja-min, and then he would know if they spoke the truth or not. Then they talked to one an-oth-er, and said that now God had done this to them for their sin when they had cast Jo-seph in the pit.

Reu-ben said to them, "Did I not say, do not sin a-gainst the child, and ye would not hear me."

Jo-seph heard them, for they thought he could not know what they said as he had spo-ken in E-gyp-tian. And he had to go from them and weep, for he loved them in spite of the wrong they had done him. But he still seemed to think they were spies. At last he said that all might go home but one. He kept Sim-e-on, and bound him, and he was to stay till they brought back Ben-ja-min.

He gave them sacks full of corn to take home, and put back their mon-ey in each sack. So they start-ed on the road home. When they stopped to rest, and one wished to give some food to his ass, he found the mon-ey. Then they were all in great fright, for they did not know how it had come there.

When they reached their home they told all to their fa-ther. How that the lord of the land had said they were spies, and they had told him they were true men, and all lived with their fa-ther in the land of Ca-naan where the youn-gest was with him. And how he had kept Sim-e-on as a pledge, and sent them home for Ben-ja-min, and had filled their sacks with corn and put their mon-ey in each sack.

Ja-cob was grieved, and said that Sim-e-on was gone, and Jo-seph was gone, and now they want-ed to take Ben-ja-min. But Reu-ben said, "Slay my two sons if I do not bring Ben-ja-min safe back to thee."

Still Ja-cob said he could not let him go.

But bread grew more scarce in the land, and when all the corn was gone that they had brought in the sacks it seemed as if they must starve. So he said, "Go down in-to E-gypt and buy us some corn."

But Ju-dah told him that if he would let Ben-ja-min go with them they would go. If not it was of no use to go, for the lord of the land had said, "Ye shall not see my face if your broth-er is not with you."

Then Ja-cob asked them why they had told the man they had a broth-er at home.

They said, "The man asked, 'Is your fa-ther a-live, and have you an-oth-er broth-er?' How could we know he would say, 'Bring your broth-er down.'"

Then Ja-cob said if it must be so he would send a gift to the lord of the land. So he gave them a lit-tle balm and hon-ey and spice and nuts, and all the mon-ey they had brought back in their sacks and as much more. And he prayed to God to keep them safe and make the man kind to them.

So they took Ben-ja-min and went down to E-gypt. And when Jo-seph saw that the boy was with them, he said that they must all come to his house. Then they were in great fear that he meant to make them his slaves.

They told the stew-ard who was at the door of Jo-seph's home how they had found the mon-ey in their sacks and had brought it back.

But he told them not to fear and he brought them wat-er to bathe their feet. And Sim-e-on who had been left bound came and met them. Then they brought out the gifts they had for Jo-seph, and bowed down to the earth when they saw him.

And he looked at Ben-ja-min and said, "Is this the youn-ger broth-er of whom ye spake to me? May God be good to thee my son!"

And Jo-seph went out and wept with joy at the sight of Ben-ja-min.

But he went back, and made them all sit down to dine, and sent them food from his own ta-ble. But Ben-ja-min's share was five times as much as any of theirs. So they ate and drank and feasted with him.

Jo-seph told his stew-ard to fill all their sacks with corn, and to put all the mon-ey back that they had brought. He said, " Put my cup, my sil-ver cup, in the sack's mouth of the youn-gest."

So as soon as it was light and they had gone a short

way, Jo-seph said to his stew-ard, "Up and aft-er them, and say, why have ye done e-vil for good?"

The man did so, and asked them why they had tak-en the sil-ver cup from which his lord drank.

Jo-seph's broth-ers were in a great state of fear when they heard this. They vowed they had no cup. They said that when their mon-ey had been found in the sacks they had brought it back. They might have kept it if they had been thieves, and now why should he think they would take sil-ver or gold that was not theirs.

· JO-SEPH RE-VEALS HIM-SELF.

They said that if the cup was found on one of them he should be put to death and all the rest would be Jo-seph's slaves. But the stew-ard said the one who took the cup should be his slave and the rest could go. So each man took the sack from the back of his ass and set it on the ground. The stew-ard looked in each in turn, and he found the cup in Ben-ja-min's sack.

Then they all rent their clothes, and turned back to the cit-y and went to Jo-seph. He seemed to think that they had stol-en the cup, and asked if they did not know he would find it out. He said, "The man in whose hand the cup is found, he shall be my ser-vant, and as for you get you up in peace to your fa-ther."

But Ju-dah begged him and said that if they went home with-out the boy their fa-ther would die; for his life was bound up with the lad's life.

And he asked Jo-seph to let him stay and serve in the place of Ben-ja-min. "For how shall I go up to my fa-ther and the lad not with me."

Then, Jo-seph could not hide what he felt. He said, "Cause all men to go out from me." So he was left with his broth-ers, and he wept a-loud, and told them who he was. He said "I am Jo-seph, your broth-er, whom ye sold in-to E-gypt."

Then they were in great fright, but he told them God had brought good out of the wrong they had done, for he had saved ma-ny lives, "So now it was not you sent me here but God."

He said food would be scarce for five years more. No

grain would be plant-ed in that time. So he said, "Make haste and go back to thy fa-ther in Ca-naan and say to him: Thus saith thy son Jo-seph, 'God hath made me lord of all E-gypt. Come down to me and thou shalt live in the best part of the land, and I will take care of thee, and thy flocks and herds, and all that thou hast.'"

Then he kissed them all and wept, for he was glad to see them, and Ben-ja-min most of all. And they kissed him and talked with him.

Pha-raoh was pleased when he heard that Jo-seph's broth-ers were there. He sent word to them that they should take wag-ons and bring their fa-ther and those of their house, and that the goods of E-gypt should be theirs, and they should live on the fat of the land.

So Jo-seph gave them wag-ons and food for the way and clothes to wear. To Ben-ja-min he gave more than the rest and three hun-dred piec-es of sil-ver. He sent his fa-ther twen-ty ass-es load-ed with bread and meat and good things.

When the men told Ja-cob all these strange things, it seemed to him that the news was too good to be true. But when he saw the gifts, and heard all the kind words, he said, "It is e-nough. Jo-seph my son yet lives. I will go and see him be-fore I die."

CHAPTER VII.

So Ja-cob left his home and set out for E-gypt. He stopped at Beer-she-ba, where his fa-ther had built an al-tar to God years be-fore, and he prayed there. And God said to him, " Fear not to go down to E-gypt, for I will make of thee a great na-tion." And God told him that when the time came for him to die Jo-seph would be at his side.

So Ja-cob sent his son Ju-dah to go and tell Jo-seph that they were on the way. Jo-seph rode out to meet his fa-ther, and clasped him in his arms, and they both wept. Ja-cob was so glad to see this son whom he had thought dead, that it seemed as if life could bring no more joy to him, and he said, " Now let me die since I have seen thy face."

Jo-seph told them that when Pha-raoh sent for them and asked what kind of work they were used to, they must say they had kept herds and flocks. Then he would let them live in Go-shen, which was a good land.

So Jo-seph brought five of his broth-ers to Pha-raoh and they spoke as he had told them. They said they had come to stay for a time in the land of E-gypt, as there was no food for them in their own home.

Pha-raoh said they might live in the land of Go-shen,

and if they had men a-mong them who could do it, they
might have the care of his cat-tle.

Then Jo-seph brought his fa-ther to Pha-raoh. And
Pha-raoh asked him how old he was. He said one hun-
dred and thir-ty years; and Ja-cob blessed Pha-raoh.

So Ja-cob and all the breth-ren and their chil-dren went
to the land of Go-shen and lived there. And Jo-seph
gave them food and all that they need-ed.

There were still more years when bread was scarce, and
the peo-ple came to Jo-seph to buy, and gave him all they
had for corn. At last they sold him all their land so that
Pha-raoh owned all E-gypt.

When the sev-en years were past they had no seed to
plant, or gold to buy it, so Jo-seph gave them seed and
told them they could pay for it with a fifth part of the
crops they raised.

So the years passed and at last Ja-cob felt that the time
of his death was near. He sent for Jo-seph and told
him that he wished to be bur-ied in his own land, and he
must take his dead bod-y there.

So Ja-cob grew worse and some one told Jo-seph,
" Thy fa-ther is sick."

Then he called his two sons, E-phra-im and Ma-nas-seh,
and they went to Ja-cob's house. His fa-ther sat up in
the bed and talked with him. He told him how God
had dealt with him and blessed him. And when he
knew that E-phra-im and Ma-nas-seh were there, he told
Jo-seph to bring the lads that he might bless them. Now
he was old and his sight was dim. He put his arms

a-round the boys and kissed them, and said he had thought he would not see Jo-seph a-gain, and now God had let him see him and his sons too.

Then he stretched out his hands and laid them on the boys' heads and blessed them. And he called all the rest of his sons and blessed each one and talked to them. He told them that God would lead them back to their own land, and that they must take his bod-y and lay him in the cave which A-bra-ham had bought, and where he had bur-ied his wife Le-ah.

So he spoke no more, but drew up his feet in the bed and died.

Jo-seph wept o-ver him and kissed him. Then he told his ser-vants that they must bring spi-ces and oth-er things which were used by the E-gyp-tians for their dead—to keep them from go-ing to dust. All the E-gyp-tians mourned for Ja-cob.

Then Jo-seph sent and told Pha-raoh that his fa-ther wished to be bur-ied in his own land, and that if he would let him go he would come back to the land of E-gypt. Pha-raoh gave him leave. So they went in great state and left the bod-y of Ja-cob in the cave where he had wished to rest.

Now that Ja-cob was dead, the broth-ers of Jo-seph feared that he would not be kind to them. They sent to him and said that their fa-ther had left word that he should for-give them. Jo-seph wept when he heard this, and when they came and fell on their fa-ces he said, " I will take care of you and your lit-tle ones." And he told them

God had meant to do good by send-ing him to E-gypt that he might save ma-ny peo-ple from starv-ing.

So they stayed on in E-gypt long years till Jo-seph's sons were grown. At last Jo-seph felt that his death was near, and he told his broth-ers that when God led them back to Ca-naan they must take his bod-y with them.

So Jo-seph died, and in the course of time all his broth-ers died too. But their chil-dren and their chil-dren's chil-dren lived still in E-gypt, and they were ma-ny.

CHAPTER VIII.

THE STO-RY OF MO-SES. — THE PLAGUES OF E-GYPT.

THERE was a new king who ruled over the land whose name was Pha-raoh, but he had not e-ven heard of Jo-seph. So when he saw that the chil-dren of Is-ra-el were so ma-ny he feared lest they might rise a-gainst him. He let the E-gyp-tians use the peo-ple in a cru-el way. They set them tasks that they could not do, and made them work like slaves.

Then the king thought of a way to make them few-er, and he made a law that all the boys should be killed as soon as they were born. But the wo-men feared God, and they let the boys live. Pha-raoh sent out word that the lit-tle boys should be drowned, but the lit-tle girls might live.

Now there was an Is-ra-el-ite named Am-ram, and God

THE HARD TASKS OF THE HE-BREWS.

gave his wife a son. The moth-er feared that some one would kill him, so she hid him for three months. Then she did not dare to keep him, so she made a lit-tle boat wov-en of the long reeds that grow in wa-ter, and she daubed it with pitch so that the ba-by would not get wet. Then she laid her boy in it and took him down to the bank of the riv-er, but she could not leave him. She hid not far off to see what would be done with him.

Now Pha-raoh's daugh-ter came down with her maids to bathe. She saw the lit-tle boat and sent one of the maids for it. The ba-by cried when she looked at it, and she had a kind heart. She was sor-ry for it and said, " This is one of the He-brew chil-dren."

Then the sis-ter of the lit-tle boy who had kept watch came and said, " May I call one of the He-brew wo-men to nurse the child for thee?" And she said " Go."

THE FIND-ING OF MO-SES.

So the sis-ter went and called the child's moth-er who was near.

Pha-raoh's daugh-ter said, "Take this child and nurse it for me and I will pay thee wa-ges."

Then his moth-er took him back to her own home with a glad heart.

But when he was old e-nough, Pha-raoh's daugh-ter sent for him and had him brought up in her own house. She called his name Mo-ses, which means, "Drawn out," for she said, "I drew him out of the wa-ter."

When he was a man he knew he was not the son of Pha-roah's daugh-ter, and he chose to go with his own peo-ple. One day he saw an E-gyp-tian strike a He-brew, and he killed the E-gyp-tian and hid him in the sand.

When he saw two of his own peo-ple in a fight, he asked them why they did so. One said, "Who made thee to rule o-ver us? Wilt thou kill me as thou didst the E-gyp-tian?" Then Mo-ses knew that his deed was known, and he was a-fraid.

When Pha-raoh heard of it he tried to kill Mo-ses, but he fled in-to the land of Mid-i-an. As he sat by a well there, he saw sev-en wo-men come to draw the wa-ter.

The shep-herds drove them off, but Mo-ses helped them draw wa-ter for their flocks. When they went home their fa-ther asked them how they came so soon, and they told him. Je-thro, their fa-ther, asked them who the man was, and said they must bring him to the house. So Mo-ses came to the house, and lived there for years, and took one of Je-thro's daugh-ters for his wife.

While he was there, Pha-raoh, the king of E-gypt, died. The Is-ra-el-ites still had hard times and they cried to God, and He heard them.

Now Mo-ses had the care of Je-thro's flocks, and he led them here and there where the best grass grew. So one day they came to a mount called Ho-reb. There

MO-SES KILLS AN E-GYP-TIAN.

was a bush in this place, and when Mo-ses looked at it he thought it was on fire. But when he went up to it, he saw that though it blazed it was not burned.

Then God spoke to him out of the bush and said, "Mo-ses." He answered, "Here am I!"

And God said, " Put thy shoes from off thy feet, for the place where-on thou stand-est is ho-ly ground."

Then Mo-ses hid his face, for he feared to look on God.

Then God said that He had heard the cries of the children of Is-ra-el, and that He would lead them out of the land of E-gypt. He told Mo-ses to go to the new king, who was named Pha-raoh like all the kings of E-gypt. He said that Mo-ses must tell him to let his peo-ple go, and that he was the one to lead them out of E-gypt. He must tell them that God would give them a new home in a land of milk and hon-ey. By this He meant that it was a good land where there was plen-ty to eat.

But Mo-ses feared to go, and said that his peo-ple would not hear him, or be-lieve that God had sent him.

Then the Lord said, "What is that in thine hand?"

Mo-ses said, " A rod."

The Lord said, "Cast it on the ground."

Mo-ses did so, and the rod turned to a snake and he feared it. But the Lord told him to take it by the tail, and when he had done so he found that it was a rod once more.

Then the Lord said, "Put thy hand now in thy bo-som."

Mo-ses did so, and found, when he drew it out, that it was white as snow. This was the sign of lep-ro-sy, a strange dis-ease. But the Lord made the hand of Mo-ses well a-gain, and He told him that he could work signs and won-ders for his peo-ple so they would trust him.

Still Mo-ses did not want to go. He told God that he could not speak well, and that some one else had bet-ter go. The Lord said He would teach him what to say. Still he did not want to go, and the Lord grew wroth with him.

Now Mo-ses had a broth-er, Aa-ron, and the Lord said that Aa-ron could speak well, and he could go with Mo-ses. He would teach them both what to say. All this time they stood by the bush that burned with fire, and the voice came out of the bush.

Then Mo-ses went back to Je-thro's house and asked leave to go and lead his peo-ple out of E-gypt as the Lord had said, and Je-thro gave him leave.

The Lord sent Aa-ron out to meet him, and he was glad and kissed him, and Mo-ses told him of all the words of God.

So Mo-ses and Aa-ron sent for the chief men of their peo-ple and spoke to them. Mo-ses showed them the signs that God had sent them, and they trust-ed him.

Then Mo-ses and Aa-ron went to Pha-raoh and asked that he would let the Is-ra-el-ites go and keep a feast, as the Lord had said.

But Pha-raoh said, 'Who is the Lord that I should o-bey Him? I know not the Lord, nei-ther will I let the chil-dren of Is-ra-el go."

Then they said, "It is God who has spo-ken. Let us go we pray thee!"

But Pha-raoh was an-gry and said they should not keep the peo-ple from their work, and he told them to go to work too.

Now the Is-ra-el-ites had to make bricks out of clay.

They did not bake the bricks then in fire as we do to make them hard. They set them out to dry in the sun. They put straw in the bricks to make them strong.

Now Pha-raoh was in such wrath that he said no one should give them straw—they must go out and get it. Yet they must make just as ma-ny bricks each day as when the straw was brought to them.

So those who set their tasks said, "Go and find straw where ye can." When night came, and they had not made so ma-ny bricks, they were beat-en. Though they worked as hard as they could, it took time to pick up the straw in the fields, and so they could not make so ma-ny bricks.

Pha-raoh said that they did not want to work, and that was why they said, "Let us go up and serve the Lord."

So some of the Is-ra-el-ites went to Mo-ses and Aa-ron and said that they had made their lives hard-er than be-fore.

Then Mo-ses told it all to the Lord, who said He would show what He would do. He told them to go to Pha-raoh once more, and if he should ask for a sign, Aa-ron must throw the rod on the ground and it would turn to a snake.

So they did so, and when Pha-raoh saw that Aa-ron's rod was turned to a snake he sent for all his wise men. They came with rods too, and when they cast them on the ground the Lord turned them to snakes, but Aa-ron's rod ate their rods.

Still Pha-raoh's heart was hard and he would not let them go.

The Lord told Mo-ses that he must go and stand by the

side of the riv-er, and when Pha-raoh passed he must say to him, "The God of the He-brews has sent me to say to thee, 'Let my peo-ple go.'"

But Pha-raoh would not.   Then the Lord told Aa-ron to strike the wa-ter with his rod.   When he had done so it grew as red as blood.   And all the ponds and streams were changed to blood, and the fish died in them, and no one could drink of the wa-ter.   And they had to set to work to dig wells.   The blood stayed in the riv-er sev-en days.

Still Pha-raoh would not let the peo-ple go.

Then the Lord sent a plague of frogs in the land.   They swarmed in all parts of it, in the hous-es and in the ov-ens where they baked bread.   They went in the house of Pha-raoh, in his bed room, and up on his bed.

So he sent for Mo-ses and Aa-ron and asked them to pray to their God to take the frogs a-way.   So Mo-ses prayed and the Lord did what he asked.   The frogs died all at once and lay in heaps through the land.   But when Pha-raoh saw the frogs were dead he would not let the peo-ple go.

Then the Lord told Aa-ron to strike the dust of the ground with his rod.   And when he had done so the dust was changed to lice that crept on the peo-ple and on all the beasts of the fields.

Still Pha-raoh made his heart hard and would not let the peo-ple go.

Then the Lord sent a plague of flies that swarmed in all the hous-es, and ov-er Pha-raoh and all his court.   But in the land of Go-shen, where the He-brews lived, there were no flies.

Then Pha-raoh sent for Mo-ses and Aa-ron and said that their peo-ple might keep a feast to their Lord, but they must not go out of the land of E-gypt. But Mo-ses told the king that they could not do this in E-gypt, for the E-gyp-tians bowed down to calves and ox-en, so if they saw one of these burnt on an al-tar they would be an-gry.

And he begged Pha-raoh to let them go out a three days jour-ney and keep their feast.

Then Pha-raoh said they might go, if they would not go far, and he asked Mo-ses to pray to their God to take off the flies.

So Mo-ses prayed and the swarm of flies went so that there was not one left.

When Pha-raoh saw this his heart grew hard and he would not let them go.

Then the Lord told Mo-ses to say to Pha-raoh that if he did not let the chil-dren of Is-ra-el go, He would kill the flocks and herds of the E-gyp-tians, but save all those of the chil-dren of Is-ra-el. But Pha-raoh did not be-lieve this, and so the cows and hor-ses and all sorts of beasts died through the whole land.

But not one of the chil-dren of Is-ra-el's flocks died. Pha-raoh sent and found out this, but strange to say it seemed to make his heart more hard and he would not let them go.

So the Lord sent a new plague to E-gypt. He told Mo-ses and Aa-ron each to take a hand-ful of ash-es and throw them up in the air in the sight of Pha-raoh. These ash-es flew like dust, and when they fell on a man or a beast they made sore boils.

Still Pha-raoh would not let them go.

Then the Lord told Mo-ses and Aa-ron to say that He would send a great storm of hail, and that each one must put his cat-tle in the barns, for if any were left out they would be killed. Some of the E-gyp-tians feared the Lord, and took in their cat-tle, but some let them stay in the fields.

And the Lord told Mo-ses to stretch out his hand to heav-en, and he did so, with his rod in it. And the hail fell, and thun-der roared, and fire ran on the ground, so that there was hail and fire mixed such as no man had seen in his life. It fell on the fields and killed ev-er-y liv-ing thing, and broke down the bush-es and trees, and spoiled all the grain. But in the land of Go-shen no hail fell.

Still Pha-raoh's heart was hard, and he would not let the peo-ple go.

Then Mo-ses said a plague of lo-custs should come on the land.

By this time the E-gyp-tians feared the wrath of God, and they went to their king and begged him to let the chil-dren of Is-ra-el go, that no more plagues should be sent on them. So the king sent for Mo-ses and Aa-ron and said, " Go and serve the Lord your God."

And he asked how ma-ny they want-ed to take with them. Mo-ses said all the chil-dren of Is-ra-el, old and young, with their flocks and herds.

But Pha-raoh said the men could go, but the wo-men and chil-dren must stay in E-gypt.

So the Lord told Mo-ses to stretch out his hand with his rod and he did so. An east wind blew all the night, and when the day came, lo-custs lay so thick on the ground that it could not be seen. They went in the king's house and in the house of ev-er-y E-gyp-tian. They ate each green thing, and all the fruit on the trees, till there was not a blade of grass left in the land.

Then Pha-raoh called Mo-ses and Aa-ron and said " I have sinned," and he begged them to for-give him this once and take a-way the lo-custs and he would be sure to let them go this time.

So Mo-ses prayed to the Lord, and a strong wind came from the west and blew all the lo-custs a-way in-to the Red Sea and they were drowned. But when Pha-raoh saw that they were gone, he would not let the peo-ple go.

So the Lord told Mo-ses to stretch forth his hand and he did so. Then it grew dark through all the land of E-gypt, so that they could not see for three days. No one dared to move out of his place the dark-ness was so great. But in the hous-es of the chil-dren of Is-ra-el it was light.

Then Pha-raoh said the peo-ple might go if they would leave all their flocks and herds.

But Mo-ses told him the flocks and herds must go too, for they need-ed them to of-fer up to the Lord. Then Pha-raoh showed great wrath and said they should not go, and if Mo-ses came to him once more he would have him killed.

Then Mo-ses told him that God would come to the land of E-gypt in the night and cause the first born in each house to die, from the first born in Pha-raoh's house down to the poor-est cot in the land There would be grief and tears through all the land for in each house there would be one dead.

On-ly in the hous-es of the chil-dren of Is-ra-el there would be no deaths.

So Mo-ses went out from Pha-raoh.

Then the Lord told the men and wo-men of the Is-ra-el-ites to ask the E-gyp-tians to lend them some of their jew-els, rings, or neck-la-ces, and such things wrought of gold and sil-ver, and they did so.

And God told Mo-ses and Aa-ron to tell each man to take a lamb and keep it four days; then to kill it in the e-ven-ing. And he must take a sprig of a plant called hys-sop and dip it in the blood and touch each side of the door of his house with it, and set one mark on the top. Then he was to stay in his house all night, and roast the lamb, and all were to eat of it. They must keep their shoes on their feet and their staves in their hands, so that they could start at once, and they must eat in haste.

The Lord meant to kill all the first-born of the E-gyp-tians that night, so that Pha-raoh would let his peo-ple go. But he would pass o-ver the hous-es that were marked with blood and no harm would come to a-ny one in them.

So they call that feast the Pass-o-ver to this day and the bread which they ate then and all that week had no yeast in it.

THE FIRST PASS-O-VER.

So Mo-ses told his peo-ple, and they did as the Lord had said.

The Lord passed through the land that night, and when He saw the marks of blood on the doors no harm came to those in that house. But in each house of the E-gyp-tians the first-born died. And there was a great cry in the night that went up through the land, for there was not a house where there was not one dead.

Then Pha-raoh sent for Mo-ses and Aa-ron and told them to make haste and go out of the land; they and their peo-ple and flocks and herds.

So the chil-dren of Is-ra-el rose and took all they owned, and all the gold and sil-ver the E-gyp-tians gave them, and set out for the land that God had prom-ised them.

CHAPTER IX.

HOW THEY CROSSED THE RED SEA.

God led the chil-dren of Is-ra-el by a long way to the land of Ca-naan. They went by the Red Sea.

And Mo-ses took the bod-y of Jo-seph with him, as he had made the chil-dren of Is-ra-el prom-ise to do.

So the Lord led them on and He showed them the way by a strange cloud that kept in front of them. In the night it was like a fire, and so they could see how to go in the dark.

Now when they were gone, Pha-raoh still was sor-ry he had let them go. They had been his slaves and made great wealth for him. So he called his troops, and start-ed out in a char-i-ot to go aft-er them.

The chil-dren of Is-ra-el had made a camp by the Red Sea; and all at once they looked and saw the ar-my of the E-gyp-tians.

Then they were in great fear and cried to the Lord. They blamed Mo-ses too, and said that they had bet-ter have stayed and worked in E-gypt than to be killed here. But Mo-ses said, "Fear not, but wait and see what the Lord will do for you. The Lord will fight for you."

So it come to pass that when Pha-raoh and his troops were near them, the pil-lar of cloud that went in front moved to the rear of them. On the side next them it was light and lighted their camp, but on the side next the E-gyp-tians it was so dark they could not see how to move, for it was night.

Then the Lord bade the chil-dren of Is-ra-el to go on. And He told Mo-ses to lift up his rod and hold it o-ver the sea and they could go o-ver on dry ground. Mo-ses did so, and the Lord sent a wind that blew the waves on each side and piled them up like a great wall. Then the ground was left dry, and the chil-dren of Is-ra-el went o-ver and did not as much as wet their feet.

When Pha-raoh saw that they were gone, he thought he could go with his troops the same way. But the Lord saw them and He made the wheels of their char-i-ots come off so that they could not drive on. And the E-gyp-tians said, "Let us go back, for the Lord fights a-gainst us."

God told Mo-ses to stretch out his hand o-ver the sea and he did so.

Then all the wa-ter came back once more, and Pha-raoh and his hosts were all drowned. Not one was left.

Mo-ses and all his peo-ple were safe, and they sang a song of praise. Then they went on for three days, and they came to a place called Ma-rah. They tast-ed the wa-ter there but it was so bit-ter they could not drink it.

PHA-RAOH AND HIS HOSTS ARE DROWNED IN THE RED SEA.

They said to Mo-ses, "What shall we drink?" Mo-ses asked the Lord, and the Lord showed him a tree and told him to throw that in the wa-ter. He did so and it made the wa-ter fit to drink.

Then they went on for some days and at last food grew scarce. The peo-ple blamed Mo-ses, and said that in E-gypt they had bread and meat to eat, and they wished he had left them there, and not brought them to this wild place to die.

The Lord heard this, and He said He would give them food to eat, and take care of them.

So when the sun was go-ing down, great flocks of quails flew in the camp, and they caught them. And in the night fell small round white things, that lay thick on the ground. They did not know what it was at first, but Mo-ses said, "This is food that the Lord has sent for you to eat."

He told each man to pick up as much as he need-ed for his house for one day, but no more, as they must trust in God who would send it as it was need-ed.

Now there were some who did not have faith, and they took more, and tried to keep it, but it was spoiled and had worms in it. When the sun grew hot, the Man-na, as it was called, melt-ed. But on the day be-fore the Sab-bath there was twice as much Man-na fell, and they could keep it, for the Lord did not want them to work on the Sab-bath. Some of them went to look for it on the Sab-bath, but they found none, and the Lord was not pleased with them.

The Man-na was small as a seed and sweet as hon-ey. Mo-ses told Aa-ron to put some in a pot and keep it to show in the years to come how the Lord had fed his peo-ple.

The chil-dren of Is-ra-el were apt to find fault with Mo-ses when they did not have what they want-ed. If wa-ter was scarce they blamed him, and said that he had brought them out of E-gypt to kill them.

And Mo-ses cried to the Lord, "What shall I do with them, for they are fit to stone me?"

Now they had reached the place called Ho-reb, where

Mo-ses had seen the bush that was on fire and did not burn, and where the Lord had told him to go and lead the chil-dren of Is-ra-el out of the land of E-gypt.

MO-SES STRIK-ING THE ROCK.

The Lord told him to strike his rod on a rock in Ho-reb and wa-ter would flow from it. Mo-ses did so, and the peo-ple drank.

Now some of the peo-ple of the land, called Am-a-lek-ites, came out to fight them. Then Mo-ses called a brave man named Josh-u-a and said to him, "Choose men and go out and fight the Am-a-lek-ites, and I will stand on the hill with the rod of God in my hand."

So Josh-u-a took some brave men and went out to the fight. Mo-ses and Aa-ron went up on a high hill, and while Mo-ses held up the rod the chil-dren of Is-ra-el won the fight. But as soon as the rod was drop-ped they lost. Now Mo-ses grew tired, and then Aa-ron and a man named Hur helped him to hold up his hands, and they kept up the rod till the sun went down and the chil-dren of Is-ra-el won the fight. God was an-gry with the Am-a-lek-ites and said the time would come when not one of them should be left in the land.

In the third month aft-er they had left E-gypt they came near a mount named Si-nai, and there they pitched their camp.

Mo-ses went up the mount, and the Lord talked with him and told that He wished to speak with him so that all the chil-dren of Is-ra-el would hear.

He told him to tell them all to bathe, and make them clean, and to do no sin, and on the third day He would come down from Mount Si-nai and speak to them. They must not go up the mount on that day or they would be sure to die. But they would hear a great trump-et blow and then they could stand at the foot of the mount.

Mo-ses told the peo-ple all this, and they did as the Lord had said. And on the third day they heard thun-der, and saw the flash of light-ning, and there was a thick

AA-RON AND HUR HOLD UP THE HANDS OF MO-SES.

cloud on the mount. Then the trum-pet sound-ed and the
peo-ple shook for fear. And all the mount seemed on fire
and it shook to its base.

Then Mo-ses spoke and God an-swered and gave the
words of ten com-mands to the peo-ple, which should
be the rules of their lives. We give them here in a short
way.

This was the first com-mand: Thou shalt have no oth-er
God be-fore me.

Sec-ond. Thou shalt not make a-ny grav-en im-age,
nor bow down to it and wor-ship it.

Third. Thou shalt not take the name of the Lord thy God in vain.

Fourth. Re-mem-ber the Sab-bath day to keep it ho-ly.

Fifth. Hon-or thy fa-ther and moth-er.

Sixth. Thou shalt not kill.

Sev-enth. Thou shalt not com-mit a-dul-ter-y.

Eight. Thou shalt not steal.

Ninth. Thou shalt not bear false wit-ness a-gainst thy neigh-bor.

Tenth. Thou shalt not cov-et a-ny-thing that is thy neigh-bor's.

Now the peo-ple heard God's voice, and they were a-fraid. They said to Mo-ses, "Speak thou with us and we will hear, but let not God speak to us or we shall die."

But Mo-ses said the Lord had spo-ken so that they would fear to sin.

And God told Mo-ses to come up on the mount once more and he would write all these laws on two ta-bles of stone. Mo-ses did so and Josh-u-a went with him. First there came a cloud that stayed on the mount six days. Then, on the sev-enth day. the Lord spoke to Mo-ses out of the cloud, and Mo-ses went up in-to the cloud. He was not seen for for-ty days, but the peo-ple saw a fire at the top of the cloud, and they felt that God was there.

The Lord told Mo-ses that the peo-ple should build a tab-er-na-cle—a house in which they might meet and pray to him. He showed him a plan of this tab-er-na-cle, which was to be rich with sil-ver and gold and fine work in brass. Mo-ses was to ask the peo-ple to bring gifts to

help this work. Then God said there must be an ark
made of wood, cov-ered out and in with gold, and in this
ark Mo-ses must keep the two ta-bles of stone that He
would give him. On the cov-er of the ark, at each end,
they must have two an-gels wrought in pure gold They
were to face each oth-er and have their wings spread.
There must be a ta-ble made of wood cov-ered with gold
to stand in the tab-er-na-cle and a gold-en can-dle-stick to
hold a light that should burn there all the time.

This tab-er-na-cle was to be made so that men could
raise it and bear it from place to place like a tent. The
wood was all to be cov-ered with gold, and rich cur-tains
were to be hung at the door, and on the in-side to make
two rooms of it. In one the ark with the law on the
ta-bles of stone was to be kept, and in one the ta-ble and
the gold-en can-dle-stick. There was to be a court a-round
this tab-er-na-cle, and there must be a large al-tar in this
court, made of wood with brass laid on it. On this al-tar
ox-en and sheep and goats were to be of-fered up to God.

And the Lord said that Aa-ron and his sons should
be priests in this tab-er-na-cle, and they should be clothed
in rich robes. Aa-ron was to be the high priest, and on
his cap of white lin-en these words were to be placed on
a gold plate, " Ho-li-ness to the Lord."

All their robes were to be of fine stuffs of blue and
scar-let and decked with pre-cious stones.

When the tab-er-na-cle was built, Mo-ses was to lead
Aa-ron and his sons there, and make them wash in pure
wa-ter. Then they were to put on the rich robes, and

Mo-ses must pour oil on Aa-ron's head, and of-fer up a lamb for him on the al-tar. And each day two lambs must be of-fered up on the great brass al-tar, one in the morn-ing and one at night, for the sins of the peo-ple.

Then there must be a small al-tar made and cov-ered with gold. It was to stand in the room where the ta-ble and can-dle-stick were.

In-cense must be burned on this al-tar. In-cense is made of the gum of a tree and has a sweet smell. We are told that the an-i-mals burnt on the brass al-tar were to show forth the death of the son of God, who died for our sins.

Then God told Mo-ses that there must be a great ba-sin of brass filled with wa-ter, to stand in the court. He named the man who should have charge of all this work.

Then He gave Mo-ses the ta-bles of stone on which He had writ-ten the ten laws with His own hands.

CHAPTER X.

THE CALF OF GOLD.

Now all this time the chil-dren of Is-ra-el were in camp at the foot of Mount Si-nai. They grew tired at last and came to Aa-ron and said, "As for this man Mo-ses who brought us up out of the land of E-gypt, we know not what has be-come of him."

And they asked Aa-ron to make an i-dol for them that they might pray to it. He told them to give him their gold rings, and they did so. He melt-ed them in the fire, and made an i-dol in the shape of a calf.

And they said this calf should be their god. Aa-ron built them an al-tar and the next day they rose up and burnt sheep on it to the calf and pray-ed to it, and had a feast there.

The Lord saw this, and told Mo-ses to go down and stop the peo-ple's sin. So he went down with the two ta-bles of stone in his hand.

When he drew near, he heard the noise of the peo-ple, and Josh-u-a said, "There is a noise of war in the camp."

But Mo-ses said that it was not the voice of those that have won and shout, nor the voice of those that have lost and cry that he heard, but it was the voice of those that sing.

And when he came near-er and saw the calf and the peo-ple that danced, he was so an-gry that he cast down the ta-bles of stone and broke them.

Then he took the calf and burnt it in the fire and ground it to dust, and he put the dust in the wa-ter the peo-ple had to drink. He asked Aa-ron why he had helped the peo-ple to sin.

Aa-ron tried to find some ex-cuse. He said the peo-ple were bent on sin, and brought him their gold rings, and he just dropped them in the fire and they took the shape of a calf.

Then Mo-ses stood in the gate, and called all those who were on the Lord's side to come to him. And he told them to go through the camp and slay those they should

MO-SES BREAKS THE TA-BLES OF THE LAW.

meet, so that they might be free of this sin. In that day there were three thou-sand slain.

Then Mo-ses said he would pray to the Lord for them, and he did so. He said, "Oh Lord, these peo-ple have sinned a great sin," and he begged God to for-give them.

But God would not; and He told them that they should not have the cloud to guide them on the way, but would have to find the land of Ca-naan as best they could. But Mo-ses prayed with all his heart, till at last the Lord said He would still go with them. And He told Mo-ses to make two ta-bles of stone and He would write once more His laws on them.

The Lord told Mo-ses that when he reached Ca-naan he must not make friends of the peo-ple who bowed down to strange gods. He must pull down their al-tars and break their i-dols. So Mo-ses went up in the mount and fast-ed for-ty days and nights. Then the Lord wrote the ten com-mand-ments on the ta-bles of stone that he had brought. Mo-ses came down with the ta-bles. And his face shone be-cause he had been with the Lord.

Then he told the peo-ple that they were to bring gifts to build a house to the Lord. So they brought gold and sil-ver and brass, or fine lin-en, or wood, just what they chose to give. They brought so much that at last Mo-ses sent word through the camp that he need-ed no more.

Then those who knew how to weave went to work and made cur-tains of fine lin-en, blue and scar-let, and they dyed goat skins to put on the roof. The cur-tain that hung on the in-side and made the two rooms was called the veil. It was of blue and pur-ple and scar-let and was very rich. And all the work was done as the Lord had said. And the rich robes for Aa-ron and his sons were wov-en with gold and set with pre-cious stones.

When all was done God told Mo-ses to set up the tab-er-na-cle and he did so. The cur-tains of fine lin-en were hung, and the al-tar was set in the court, and the great ba-sin near the al-tar where Aa-ron and his sons could wash their feet and hands.

Then when all was done the pil-lar of cloud that went

be-fore them to show the way came o-ver the ta-ber-na-cle, and stayed there, and it was all filled with the glo-ry of God.

The Lord spoke to Mo-ses from that place, and gave him all the new laws for the chil-dren of Is-ra-el.

CHAPTER. XI.

GOD GIVES MORE LAWS.

God told Mo-ses to bring Aa-ron and his sons so that they might be made His priests. So Mo-ses called the peo-ple, and then he brought Aa-ron and his sons, and they were washed with wa-ter and put on the rich robes that had been made for them. They were to stay near the tab-er-na-cle, and go in and burn in-cense and of-fer up gifts to the Lord.

When Aa-ron had been made high priest, he took a lamb and killed it, and laid it on the al-tar. Then the Lord sent fire and burned the lamb. All the peo-ple shout-ed for joy when they saw the fire, for they knew the Lord was pleased with them. They kept the fire burn-ing on the al-tar all the time, be-cause the Lord had sent it.

Each day two lambs were of-fered up on that al-tar, one in the morn-ing and the oth-er at night. There were two kinds of of-fer-ing; one when a man grieved for his sin, and brought an an-i-mal which was laid on the al-tar by the priest and burnt up. This was called a burnt of-fer-ing.

Then when a man wished to give thanks to God, or to ask Him to bless him, the priests did not burn the an-i-mal all up. They kept part to eat, and they gave some to the man to eat. This kind was known as a peace of-fer-ing.

The man would take his part home, and call in his friends to eat with him, and they would keep a feast. For he had to eat it all that day, it must none of it be kept.

Aa-ron and his sons must burn in-cense each day. They put coals in a sort of cup, and the cup was set on the al-tar, and then the gum was strewn on the coals so that a sweet smoke went up. They must take the coals from the al-tar where God had sent the fire. It burned night and day.

Once two of Aa-ron's sons took strange fire for their in-cense, and God was an-gry, so they were burnt to death. Mo-ses said that no one should mourn for them, as they had died for their sins.

And God told Mo-ses what an-i-mals and beasts and birds the peo-ple might eat when they reached the land of Ca-naan. They might not eat cam-els or rab-bits or pigs. They could eat all fish that had scales on it, but those that were smooth they must not eat. That which they could eat was called clean, and the rest was un-clean.

Now there was a strange dis-ease in that land called lep-ro-sy. God told Mo-ses that when a man had a spot or sore on him he must go at once to the priest. If he had lep-ro-sy, he must go out of the camp far from men and live till he grew well. Then he must go back to the priest and let him see if he was well. If he were well he could go back in the camp, but he must bring three lambs, or if he were too poor for that, he must bring one lamb or a pair of doves to of-fer up as thanks to God who had cured him.

Now God meant to teach His peo-ple by all these things. The high priest prayed for the peo-ple as Christ does for us in Heav-en.

The Lord said that when the chil-dren of Is-ra-el should have their homes in Ca-naan, and have fields and fruit-trees, they must leave some grain in the field and fruit on the tree for the poor in the land who had none.

They must not steal or lie, and must pay each day the men who worked for them. They must not speak a-gainst a deaf man who could not hear, or put a stone in the way of the blind, and they must not tell tales of each oth-er. They must love each oth-er and speak kind words. If they saw one sin they must tell how wrong it was and try to lead him to do right. They must treat those who came from oth-er lands as though they were friends.

Now the peo-ple where they were go-ing prayed to an i-dol made of brass, with the face of a calf, called Mo-loch. It was hol-low on the in-side, so that a fire could be made in it. When the fire had made it hot they used to put their ba-bies in the i-dol's arms and they were burnt to death. Then they beat drums so that they would not hear the cries of the poor chil-dren.

Now God told Mo-ses that if one of the chil-dren of Is-ra-el should give his child to Mo-loch, he must be stoned till he was dead. If they did not kill him, God would do it.

The Lord told them they must keep three feasts a year to Him. The first was the feast of the pass-o-ver, which was first kept at the time when they were to go out of E-gypt, and the Lord had passed o-ver their hous-es and slain the first born of the E-gyp-tians. They must eat bread with no yeast in it for sev-en days, so that they would think of the way in which the Lord had made Pha-raoh let them go.

Sev-en weeks aft-er the pass-o-ver they must keep the feast of the har-vest for one day when all the grain had been put in the barns. This was to thank God that He had made it to grow.

When all the grain was brought in and the fruit picked they were to keep a feast for sev-en days. They were to cut off branch-es of trees and make booths or tents of them so that they would not for-get how they had lived in tents, and the way the Lord had led them in the des-ert.

The Lord said they must bring ol-ive oil to burn in the lamps in His tab-er-na-cle all night and all day, and that no one but the priests should trim these lamps.

And He said they must have twelve loaves made of fine flour, and place them on the gold-en ta-ble in His tab-er-na-cle. When it had been there a week Aa-ron or his sons must take it out and put new bread there. They might eat the old bread, but they must eat it in the Lord's house be-cause it was ho-ly bread. They might not take it home.

There was a man in the camp who spoke e-vil of God at this time, and the Lord told Mo-ses that they must put him to death. So the man was sent out of the camp and stoned till he died.

The Lord said that when they reached Ca-naan they might plant and reap for six years and take all that grew, but the sev-enth year they should let the land rest and not plant it. They need not fear that they should have no food to eat, for He would make twice as much to grow in the sixth year.

Once in fif-ty years there was to be a time of great joy. It was to be called the year of ju-bi-lee. They were to do no work that year, but God would give them food. If a poor man had lost or sold his land he should get it back in that year and all that were slaves must be set free.

If they would keep all his laws God prom-ised His peo-ple that they would thrive in their new homes. Their crops would grow, and no wild beast should hurt them. No foe could harm them, for He would take care of them. But if they sinned they should not thrive. Their grain should not grow and wild beasts would take off their chil-dren and kill their flocks. They should die in the streets for want of food and their foes would make war on them and take them for slaves.

Yet if those who were left were sor-ry for their sins, and prayed to Him, He would be their friend once more.

CHAPTER XII.

THE chil-dren of Is-ra-el were now twelve tribes, and God told Mo-ses to count them. Each tribe came from one of the sons of Ja-cob. All of these but the Le-vites were to give men to fight the foes whom they would meet on the way. But the Le-vites had the care of the house of God. They had to wait on Aa-ron and his sons.

Now the pil-lar of cloud was still o-ver this house, and in the night it shone like fire. When it moved they knew that the Lord meant that they should go on.

When they moved they marched like troops and bore ban-ners. Each tribe kept its own place and had a cap-tain. When they stopped, the house of the Lord was set down first. Then the Le-vites pitched their tents near it.

Now the time came for them to leave Mount Si-nai, and the Lord spoke to them and told them to go on. The cloud moved and they start-ed out on their march. They went for three days and stopped at Pa-ran.

There they found fault with the Lord. They said they were tired of Man-na and want-ed meat. In E-gypt, they said, they had fish and meat and all sorts of good things, and they were sick of the Man-na. And they wept in their tents.

Mo-ses felt very much cast down. He asked God why He had giv-en him the care of such peo-ple. It was too

much for him, and he would rath-er die that go on with it.
The Lord said to him that he should tell the peo-ple they
should have meat, more than they want-ed. They should
have it for a whole month till they could not bear the
sight of it. Then Mo-ses said, " Here are six hun-dred
thous-and peo-ple and Thou say-est that Thou wilt give
them flesh that they may eat for a whole month? Must
all the flocks and herds be killed, or all the fish of the sea
be caught?"

And the Lord said " Hath My hand grown weak, that
I can-not do it? Wait and thou shalt see."

Mo-ses told the peo-ple what the Lord had said. And
great winds blew so that quails fell thick a-round the camp
and lay in heaps on the ground. The peo-ple went and
picked them up for two days.

But while they ate, the Lord sent a plague on them for
their sins, and ma-ny died.

Now when they had gone on for a time it came in-to
the heart of Aa-ron and of Mir-i-am, the sis-ter of Mo-ses,
to find fault with him. Mir-i-am said that the wife of
Mo-ses was not one of the chil-dren of Is-ra-el, and that
he had no right to rule them.

Then the Lord was wroth with Mir-i-am and Aa-ron,
and He bade them go to the door of the tab-er-na-cle.
And the Lord came in the pil-lar of cloud and told them
that Mo-ses did His will, and asked if they did not fear
to speak a-gainst him.

When the cloud rose from that place Aa-ron looked at
Mir-i-am and saw she was a le-per as white as snow. .

And he cried out to Mo-ses, "We have sinned," and he prayed that Mir-i-am might be healed. And the Lord had pit-y on her and healed her.

At last the long march drew near its end. The chil-dren of Is-ra-el were near to Ca-naan. They thought best to send out spies to see the land first and bring back word of all they saw. So Mo-ses chose twelve men, one from each tribe, to go and see if it were a good land, and what sort of peo-ple lived in it. He want-ed to know if they had strong cit-ies with walls a-round them, or if they lived in tents, and he told the spies to bring back some of the fruit of the land.

So the men went out and walked through Ca-naan, and the Lord kept them from all harm. They found it was a good land. The grapes at a place called Esh-col grew in bunch-es so large that it took two men to car-ry one bunch. They cut one off and tied it to a pole and each man took an end and so they brought it to show Mo-ses. They brought figs too and oth-er fruit.

They were gone for-ty days and then they came back and showed what they had brought. They said the soil was rich and grain and vines grew well. There were walled cit-ies there, and the peo-ple were strong and to be feared, and the Is-ra-el-ites had bet-ter not go there.

But there were two of the spies, Ca-leb and Josh-u-a, who had faith in God and knew He would take care of them in the strange land. They begged the peo-ple to go on, but the Is-ra-el-ites were a-fraid, and wept, and said, "We wish God had let us die in E-gypt and not brought

THE SPIES BRING BACK FRUITS FROM CA-NAAN.

us here." And they asked, "Why has the Lord brought us to this land so that we and our wives and chil-dren may be killed."

And they said, "Let us choose a new man to lead us, and go back to E-gypt." .

Then Mo-ses and Aa-ron were in deep grief. Josh-u-a and Ca-leb, the two good spies, did what they could and said that Ca-naan was a rich land and they need not fear that the Lord would not help them. But the peo-ple were in such a state that they want-ed to stone them.

Then the Lord was an-gry with the chil-dren of Is-ra-el,

and said He would send a sore sick-ness and sweep them from the face of the earth. But Mo-ses prayed to the Lord and said that if He slew his peo-ple all the na-tions would say that He could not bring them to the land as He had said and they would be glad.

The Lord said that He would not sweep them from the face of the earth, but they could not go in Ca-naan yet for their sins. They must turn back in the des-ert and wait for-ty years more. By that time all the men who had said they would not go in-to Ca-naan would be dead, and He would lead the rest there and give the land to them. And He said that the two good spies, Ca-leb and Josh-u-a, should live till then and go in-to the land.

Then the chil-dren of Is-ra-el want-ed to go to Ca-naan at once, but Mo-ses said that they could not do so now, for the Lord would not help them and the men of the land would kill them. But some did not be-lieve this, and they tried to go in-to Ca-naan, but they were chased back to their camp. So they had to turn back to the des-ert.

At one time they found a man at work on the Sab-bath, pick-ing up sticks, and they took him and kept him to see what the Lord would have them do with him. He had brok-en God's law. The Lord said to Mo-ses, " The man shall sure-ly be put to death. Take him out of the camp and stone him with stones till he is dead." And the peo-ple did as the Lord said.

There were three men named Ko-rah, Da-than, and A-bi-ram that tried to set the tribes a-gainst Mo-ses and Aa-ron. Ko-rah was a Le-vite and his work was to wait on the priests. He said Aa-ron had no more right to be high priest than he had. Mo-ses told them that they might each take a cens-er the next day, and burn in-cense on it as the priests did, and the Lord would show whom He would have for high priest. So the three men and all those they had made to think as they did went the next day and took cens-ers and put fire in them.

The Lord was an-gry with these men and He caused the ground to o-pen, and they fell down in it, and were bur-ied a-live, and their cries went up in the ears of the peo-ple. Then they feared God and fled.

Yet still some of the chil-dren of Is-ra-el talked a-gainst Mo-ses and Aa-ron, and said it was their fault that Ko-rah, Da-than, and A-bi-ram and all the men with them had been killed. They said the men who had died were good men. Then God was so an-gry with the peo-ple that He said to Mo-ses and Aa-ron, "Go from them that I may de-stroy them."

But Mo-ses and Aa-ron fell on their fa-ces and begged the Lord to spare them.

Yet while they prayed, word was brought that there was a great sick-ness in the camp and some were dead.

Then Mo-ses said to Aa-ron, "Go quick-ly and take a cens-er and put fire in it and burn in-cense to the Lord."

And Aa-ron ran out and stood with the in-cense be-tween those who had died and those who still lived, and the Lord stopped the plague. Then the Lord told Mo-ses to ask each tribe to send a rod to him, with the name of the man who brought it on it. Then he must take them to

the tab-er-na-cle and lay them in the most ho-ly place be-
fore the ark all night. He said one should bud in the
night and bear blos-soms like a tree. And the man whose
name was on that rod should be the high priest.

So the peo-ple did so. Next day when Mo-ses looked
at the rods it was found that Aa-ron's rod had bloomed
and borne al-monds. So the Lord told Mo-ses to keep
that rod in the tab-er-na-cle, so that all might know that
He chose Aa-ron for His high priest. When Aa-ron
should die, his sons were to be priests and so on, and the
Le-vites must wait on the priests, and all the oth-er tribes
must give the Le-vites part of their grain and fruit and
flocks and herds. You see the Le-vites could not earn
gold, but had to work for the Lord's house all the time, so
the rest were to give a tenth part of their goods to them.

Then the chil-dren of Is-ra-el went on till they came to
Zin and Mir-i-am died and was bur-ied there.

Once more they cried out a-gainst Mo-ses and Aa-ron,
for there was no wa-ter in the place. They said "Why
have you brought us here to die? No figs or vines grow
here, and there is no wa-ter to drink."

Then the Lord told Mo-ses to call the peo-ple to a rock
that was there. And Mo-ses felt an-gry, and he said,
"Hear now ye reb-els, must we fetch wa-ter out of this
rock for you?"

And he struck the rock with his rod twice and the
wa-ter gushed out. But God was not pleased with Mo-
ses, for he had talked as if he made the wa-ter come,
when it was God's work. And God told Mo-ses and

Aa-ron that they should not see the land of Ca-naan. They would both have to die be-fore the time came for the chil-dren of Is-ra-el to go in that land.

Now they came to the land of E-dom and Mo-ses sent to ask the king of the place if they could pass through. He told what a hard time they had in E-gypt, and now he said, " Let us pass through the land. We will not go through the fields or tread down the grain, nor will we drink the wa-ter of the wells. We will go on the king's high-way."

But the king said they should not go through his land, and he brought men out to fight them. So they turned and did not go that way.

Then they came to a mount called Hor. And God made known to Mo-ses that Aa-ron must die there on the top of the mount. The Lord said, " Take Aa-ron and his son, E-le-a-zar, and bring them to the top of the mount, and take the high priest's robes from off Aa-ron and put them on his son." And Mo-ses did so. Then Aa-ron died, and all the tribes mourned for him for-ty days.

The long march still went on, and the chil-dren of Is-ra-el sinned and said, " We loathe this Man-na, and there is no bread or wa-ter."

The Lord was not pleased with them and He sent a plague of fi-e-ry snakes in the camp that bit them so that some of them died. Then once more they begged Mo-ses. to pray God to take the plague from them. " We have sinned," they cried.

Mo-ses did pray for them, and the Lord told him to

. THE BRASS SNAKE HEALS THOSE THAT HAVE BEEN BIT-TEN.

make a brass snake and put it on a pole, and if those who
were bit-ten would look at it they should be made well.
So Mo-ses did as the Lord said, and those who were
bit-ten were healed by the Lord.

When the chil-dren of Is-ra-el reached the land of Mo-
ab, their king was named Ba-lak. Now he feared them,
and thought they had come to fight him, and he saw that
they were a great host. There was a man in his land,
named Ba-laam, who made out that he had great pow-er
with God. The king sent for this man, and told him that

if he would pray for a curse to fall on the chil-dren of Is-
ra-el he would make him rich and great.

Now Ba-laam was a rich man. but he loved gold and
he did not care how he made it. So he rose and took his
ass and set out with the men to go to the king.

Now God was wroth with Ba-laam, and He sent an
an-gel that stood right in his way with a drawn sword.
Ba-laam did not see him. but the ass did. and she turned
out of the road. He struck her but she would not go on.
She pressed up to the wall at the side of the road and
crushed Ba-laam's foot. He struck her once more and
then she fell down in the road in great fear.

Then Ba-laam beat her with his staff and the Lord made
the ass speak and say. "What have I done that thou hast
struck me these three times?"

Ba-laam told her that she had turned out of the way.
and he said. "I wish I had my sword in my hand for
now would I kill thee."

And the ass spoke once more and asked. "Have I ever
done so be-fore?" Ba-laam had to say. "No."

And the Lord caused him to see the an-gel that stood
in the road with a sword in his hand.

Then Ba-laam bowed down his face to the ground. The
an-gel said. "Why hast thou struck thine ass these three
times?"

And he told him that he had come out to stop him on
the way to sin. and that if the beast had not turned out
of the road Ba-laam would have been killed and the ass
saved.

The an-gel said that Ba-laam might go with the men, but he must speak to the king what he would tell him to say.

So he went on and the king came out to meet him. The next day the king took him up to a high place where he could look down on the camp of Is-ra-el.

AN AN-GEL STOPS BA-LAAM IN THE ROAD.

Ba-laam told the king to build sev-en al-tars, and get sev-en bulls or rams, to of-fer up.

The king did so, and burnt the beasts on the al-tar, while Ba-laam went to see if the Lord would let him curse the chil-dren of Is-ra-el. But the Lord sent him back and said he must speak good things of them, and not curse them.

But Ba-laam still want-ed to earn the gold and hoped

that in some way he might do it. And he made the king build sev-en more al-tars, and burn sev-en more beasts on them, but still the Lord said he must not curse Is-ra-el but bless them.

And a third time they tried the same thing. Then the king was wroth with Ba-laam. He said, " I sent for thee to curse my foes, and, lo, thou hast blessed them these three times." And he told him to go back to his home.

Still Ba-laam hoped for some of the gold and sought for a way to earn it. He told the Mo-ab-ites to make a feast to their i-dols and get the chil-dren of Is-ra-el to come to it. They did so, and the Is-ra-el-ites came and bowed down to the false gods. Then the Lord was wroth with them, and sent a plague that killed many of them.

When the for-ty years were passed God brought them near Ca-naan once more.

The Lord said that Mo-ses and E-le-a-zar must count the peo-ple and see how ma-ny were fit to go to war. And they found that all those who had said they would not go in-to Ca-naan the first time were dead. But the two good spies, Ca-leb and Josh-u-a, lived yet as the Lord had said.

The Lord told Mo-ses that he must send out men to fight the Mid-i-an-ites, who had led his peo-ple to bow down to false gods. So they went forth, and the Lord made them gain the fight, and they slew hosts of the foe. They took their goods and burnt their towns with fire. When they came back they found that not one of their own men had been slain. The gold and gems won from the foe were placed in the Lord's house and left there.

Then the Lord led the peo-ple to the banks of the riv-er Jor-dan. Then two of the tribes came to Mo-ses and told him they wished to stay where they were as it was a good land, and they had ma-ny flocks and herds. They did not want to go in-to Ca-naan.

Mo-ses was not pleased with them for he thought they feared to fight the men of Ca-naan. And he said, "Shall your breth-ren go o-ver to war while you rest here." They said, "We will build sheep folds for our sheep here and hous-es to live in, but we who are men will go o-ver Jor-dan and help fight the na-tions and drive them out, but when that is done we will come back and have our homes on this side of the riv-er." Then Mo-ses said they might do this, and the land they liked was called Gil-e-ad.

So these two tribes of Reu-ben and Gad built sheep folds and hous-es in Gil-e-ad, and half the tribe of Man-as-seh made their homes there too.

The Lord told Mo-ses that when the chil-dren of Is-ra-el went in-to Ca-naan, they must drive out the peo-ple and cast down all the false gods and take the land for their own. Each man was to have a piece of land where he might build, and plant grain, and feed his flocks. They must not let one of those who bowed down to false gods live, lest they might be led in-to sin. Then the Lord would drive them out as He now meant to do with those who did not serve him.

The Lord named the men who were to give each tribe its share of land. The Le-vites were to have no land, but cit-ies were giv-en them to live in.

CHAPTER XIII.

THE DEATH OF MOSES.

Mo-ses knew that he could not lead the peo-ple in-to the land of Ca-naan. He must die as the Lord had said, for he had sinned at the rock. He feared the Is-ra-el-ites would not think of how they had been led through the des-ert. He talked to them for the last time and brought back to their minds all the things God had done for them.

He asked the Lord to choose a man to take his place, lest if they had no guide to lead them they might be lost as sheep with no shep-herd. The Lord said Josh-u-a should lead them.

Mo-ses told the peo-ple they must keep the laws of God and teach their chil-dren to do so at all times; and they must talk to them of God, so that they would learn to love Him.

And when the Lord led them in-to Ca-naan and gave them all the great cit-ies that they had not built, and wells that they had not digged, and vine yards and o-live trees which they had not plant-ed, they must think of the Lord and how much He had done for them. He had led them for long years and fed them, and their clothes had not grown old and their feet had not been sore by the way. He had brought them out of that place to this good land full of streams, where the wheat grew and grapes and all sorts of fruit. They should not want. They would find brass and i-ron if they dug in the ground and could make tools and all sorts of things for their use.

Their flocks and herds would do well in that land, and they would grow rich, but they must not think they had gained all these things by their own might. They must keep in mind that the Lord their God had giv-en them all. If they did not serve Him, but took oth-er gods, they would be served in the same way as He meant to serve the na-tions that lived in sin.

Mo-ses told them they must soon cross the Jor-dan and the Lord would lead them. The peo-ple of the land might try to keep them out but He would make them win. Though they had sinned in the des-ert, He was still their God.

The land of Ca-naan was a place of streams. E-gypt had one riv-er, the Nile, which flowed o-ver its banks once a year so that the fields near it bore much fruit. But the soil far off was dry, and men had to car-ry wa-ter to it, so that the grass and plants might grow. In Ca-naan rain fell and corn and wheat and grass grew well, and vines and all sorts of fruit were found there.

The peo-ple of Ca-naan had set up their false gods on hills and un-der trees in all parts of their land. They had built al-tars and burnt up their own chil-dren on them. Mo-ses told the chil-dren of Is-ra-el that they must pull down all these pla-ces and break the false gods. And if one of the men of the land should try to make them kneel down to these false gods, he must be stoned to death.

If there was a poor man a-mong them, they must lend him what he need-ed and the Lord would bless them.

They must keep some cit-ies where one who had killed a man by chance might hide. If he had meant to kill the man for hate, then he must be put to death. But if the thing was done by chance, and the friends of the dead man chased him to kill him, he might fly to one of these cit-ies.

When he reached the gate, he must tell the guard what he had done. Then they would give him a place to stay. If the friends of the man whom he had killed came to ask for him, they would not give him up, as he had not meant to do wrong. But if a man who meant to kill came there, they were not to let him in, but he must be put to death for his sin.

When they lived in the land each man must take the first of his grain and the first fruit that was ripe and bring them to the Lord's house. The priest would take these gifts and set them down in front of the al-tar. The man must say, "I have brought the first fruits of the land which Thou, O Lord, hast giv-en me." And he must pray to the Lord and leave all his gifts there for the use of the priests.

The priests were to have no fields to raise grain or fruit of their own, so the first fruits of the land must be brought to them each year.

Mo-ses told them that on the day they should go o-ver Jor-dan they must raise a great pile of stones, and on these they must smear soft clay, and write all the laws of

God on this clay. When it grew hard, all who went by
could read the law of God on it.

Mo-ses told them that if they kept the law of God,
He would bless them and all that was theirs. Their foes
would flee from them. But if they sinned, their fields
should not bring forth grain, for lo-custs should eat it, and
their vines would not bring forth grapes. He would send
plagues on them and foes who would not spare them but
would make them slaves.

Mo-ses said he had now set two ways be-fore them, and
he begged them to take the good way so that they might
live. He told them he could not go with them in-to that
land, but Josh-u-a would lead them. And he called Josh-
u-a and told him. Then the Lord came in a pil-lar of
cloud and said that Josh-u-a was to lead his peo-ple when
Mo-ses should die.

Then Mo-ses wrote down all the laws which God had
giv-en him in a book, and he said they must be read loud
to all the peo-ple once in sev-en years.

He gave the book to the Le-vites, that it might be kept
in the ark.

Then God spoke to Mo-ses, and told him to go up to
the top of a high mount called Ne-bo. From this place
he could see the land of Ca-naan. There he died, and the
Lord bur-ied him in the land of Mo-ab. No one knew
where his grave was made:

> " For the angels of God up-turned the sod
> And laid the dead man there!"

He was one hun-dred and twen-ty years old when he

THE LORD SHOWS MO-SES THE LAND OF CA-NAAN.

died, yet the Lord had kept him strong and well all that time.

Then Josh-u-a led the chil-dren of Is-ra-el, and the Lord made him wise, so that he could guide them in the right way. But God did not talk with him face to face as He had done with Mo-ses.

CHAPTER XIV.

THE Lord's word came to Josh-u-a that he should lead the chil-dren of Is-ra-el in-to the land of Ca-naan. He would help them and they need not fear their foes if they kept His law.

So Josh-u-a said to his chief men, " Go through the camp and tell the peo-ple to take food for three days, for they shall pass o-ver Jor-dan."

And he sent two spies to look at the land. They crossed the stream to a town called Jer-i-cho and stopped at the house of a wo-man named Ra-hab.

Then some one told the king of this, and he sent to the house and said that Ra-hab must bring out the men. But the wo-man took them up to the roof of the house and hid them un-der some flax that had been left there to dry.

So they were not found. Ra-hab told the men she had heard how the Lord had made the chil-dren of Is-ra-el cross the Red Sea on dry ground, and how He had helped them in the fight with their foes. She knew that God would give them the land, and she begged that when they came to take the cit-y of Jer-i-cho they would think of her, and save her life and the lives of those who were dear to her.

The men said they would do this if she would tell no one what she knew of them.

They told her she must tie a red cord to the win-dow of
her house, so they would know it when they came in to
take the town.   Then no one in it should be harmed.

Now her house stood near the wall of the town, and it
was high, so that there was a win-dow o-ver the wall.   The
gates of the town were shut by the king so that they could
not go out.   But Ra-hab let them down by a cord out-
side the wall, and told them to hide for three days in a

RA-HAB AIDS THE SPIES TO ES-CAPE.

mount-ain near by, till the king's men gave up the search. This they did, and then went back to Josh-u-a and told him all that had passed.

Then Josh-u-a and all the peo-ple rose up at dawn and came to the bank of the riv-er. They stayed there three days and then Josh-u-a said that they would start the next day and the Lord would do great things for them.

"For the priests shall car-ry the ark o-ver Jor-dan be-fore you, and it shall be that as soon as their feet stand in the riv-er the wa-ter shall cease to flow and the priests shall walk o-ver on dry ground."

All came to pass as Josh-u-a had said. The priests took up the ark, and all the peo-ple went aft-er. As soon as their feet touched the wa-ter it part-ed and made a dry path for them all to go o-ver.

And when they were all on the oth-er side, the riv-er flowed back as be-fore.

They made their camp at a place called Gil-gal, and found some corn there which they parched and ate. Then the Man-na ceased. The Lord had sent it to them when they were in the des-ert, but now they were in a land where grain grew and they did not need it. Josh-u-a went out of the camp to look at the land, and came near to the walls of Jer-i-cho. And he saw a man on the wall with a drawn sword in his hand.

And Josh-u-a spoke to him and asked, "Art thou for us or for our foes?"

The man said, "As cap-tain of the Lord's ar-my am I come."

Then Josh-u-a bowed down to the earth for he knew that the Lord spoke to him.

The gates of the cit-y were shut, so that they could not go in, but the Lord told Josh-u-a in what way he could take the cit-y. Their men of war must march round the cit-y once a day for six days, and the priests must bear the ark with them.

Sev-en more priests must blow on ram's horns. The sev-enth day they were to march sev-en times, and the priests were to blow on the trump-ets made of ram's horns a great blast. When they heard this they must shout with all their might, and the walls of the cit-y would fall down so they could go in.

The Lord said that all the peo-ple of the cit-y must be put to death but the wo-man who had hid the spies and her fam-i-ly. All the gold and gems and spoils they found must be giv-en to the Lord. No man could keep what he found for his own or the Lord would pun-ish him.

So the peo-ple did as the Lord said. On the sev-enth day, when they marched round the cit-y for the last time, the priests blew on the ram's horns and Josh-u-a said, " Shout for the Lord has giv-en you the cit-y ! "

Then a great shout went up, and the walls of the cit-y fell flat, and they went in and took it. And Josh-u-a sent the spies to bring out all that were in Ra-hab's house so that they should be safe. Then he took all the sil-ver and gold and put it in the ark of the Lord and burned the cit-y.

Josh-u-a then sent out his spies to look at the next town

THE FALL OF THE WALLS OF JER-I-CHO.

which was called Ai. They came back and told him it was a small place and a few men could take it. So Josh-u-a sent a small force, but the men of Ai came out and fought them and killed some of them and the rest fled.

When Josh-u-a heard this he rent his clothes and bowed down his face to the earth for grief. He cried to the Lord, and said, " All the peo-ple of Ca-naan will hear how the chil-dren of Is-ra-el have fled, and they will kill us."

The Lord told him to rise. He said that the chil-dren

of Is-ra-el had sinned, and that was why they could not win the fight. One of them had hid some of the sil-ver and gold he had found in Jer-i-cho, in place of giv-ing it to the Lord. That man must be burned with fire, with all that he had, or the Lord would not help them. So Josh-u-a rose up ear-ly, and called out all the peo-ple, and the Lord showed him the man who had done this thing. His name was A-chan. Josh-u-a said, "Do not hide what thou hast done. Tell me!"

The man said.that he had seen a rich robe in Jer-i-cho, and some gold coin, and he had hid them in the ground un-der his tent.

Then Josh-u-a sent men to A-chan's tent, and they found the things where they were hid. And they brought them to Josh-u-a, who took them.

Then A-chan and his sons and daugh-ters were stoned to death, and then burned with his tent and the beasts he owned. A great heap of stones was raised to show the place. Then the Lord helped the chil-dren of Is-ra-el once more and said, "Fear not, for I will give thee the cit-y of Ai and the king of that land."

The Lord said they must put all the peo-ple to death for their sins, but they could keep the sil-ver and gold they found there.

So Josh-u-a chose some brave men whom he sent to hide at the back of the town of Ai while the rest marched with him to the front.

The king saw him, and took his troops out of the town to fight him. Then the men from the rear marched in

and set the cit-y on fire. So the men of Ai had the fire
at the back of them and Josh-u-a's troops in front of
them. They could not fly and they were all put to death
as the Lord had said.

And Josh-u-a built an al-tar of stones near there on a
mount-ain, and he put clay on it and wrote on it the laws
of God. All the men of the land heard how they had
dealt with Ai, and met to see what could be done. There
was one cit-y named Gib-e-on where they thought of a way
they might keep from war. They put on old clothes and
worn out shoes and took stale bread with them, as if they
had come a long way. When they reached the camp of
Josh-u-a, they said to him, "We live far from Ca-naan,
and we have heard the great things that God has done
for you. We wish that you would be our friends."

Now Josh-u-a did not ask the Lord what he must do,
but said at once that they would be friends. When he
heard that they had told lies, he sent for them and asked
them why they had done this thing. They said they
feared for their lives. So Josh-u-a could not put the peo-
ple of Gib-e-on to death, as he had told them they should
live, but he made slaves of them. They had to work for
the priests and car-ry wa-ter and cut wood for the al-tar.

There were five kings who called out troops to fight the
peo-ple of Gib-e-on, be-cause they had made friends with
Josh-u-a. But the men of Gib-e-on begged Josh-u-a to
come to their help, and he did so with all the men of war.
And the kings and their troops fled, and the Lord sent
great hail-stones down on them, so that ma-ny were killed.

But while they fled it grew more dark, for it was time for the sun to set. Jósh-u-a thought they would get off in the night, so he spoke to the sun and bade it not go down. And the sun stood still, and that was a long day. God

JOSH-U-A BIDS THE SUN TO STAND STILL.

let the sun shine so that they could see their foes. At last the kings and their men hid in a great cave. When Josh-u-a heard of this he said, "Roll great stones to the mouth of the cave, and set men to watch it, while you go on and find the rest of the foe."

When they came back the five kings were brought out and put to death. Then the sun went down, and the dead bod-ies were cast back in-to the cave, and great stones rolled in the mouth of it.

Then Josh-u-a cast lots for the tribes to see what part of land each might have.

And he chose cit-ies of ref-uge, and some for the priests and Le-vites to have for their own. Now the two tribes and a half that were to live in Gil-e-ad had fought all this time with the chil-dren of Is-ra-el, and had a share of all the spoil won in the war. They were rich and Josh-u-a told them that he would now give them leave to go to their homes. But they were to take care to keep God's laws and serve him.

So the men went back, and when they came to the bank of the riv-er they built a great al-tar there, shaped like the one in the ark of God. Now God had said they must have no oth-er al-tar than the one He had caused them to build. So the chil-dren of Is-ra-el sent a priest to know why these tribes had done this thing. They said they did not mean to sin, but had raised this al-tar for fear that in the days to come it might be thought that they did not be-long to the chil-dren of Is-ra-el. The al-tar was to show that they had a right to go o-ver the riv-er and pray with the rest to the God of Is-ra-el.

Then Phin-e-as the priest, and the princes were glad, and went back and told the rest all these things.

Now Josh-u-a felt that his end was near and he called his peo-ple to him, and told them how good the Lord had been.

They had the land to live in, and all its cit-ies and fields and woods. Josh-u-a said, " Fear the Lord and serve Him. Choose this day whom ye will serve, but as for me and my house, we will serve the Lord."

The peo-ple said, " God for-bid that we should leave the Lord to serve i-dols. For it was He who brought us up out of E-gypt and gave us this land. There-fore will we al-so serve the Lord for He is our God."

Then Josh-u-a took a great stone and set it up by the ark of the Lord to keep them in mind of what they had said.

Then it came to pass that Josh-u-a died, and they made his grave in the part of the land that was his own. The dead bod-y of Jo-seph which they had brought from E-gypt, they laid in the grave at She-chem.

CHAPTER XV.

GID-E-ON AND THE FLEECE.

THE chil-dren of Is-ra-el did not drive out all the peo-ple of the land as the Lord had said. And God was not pleased with them and said, " I will not drive them out a-ny more from be-fore you, but those that are left will stay in the land and tempt you to sin."

They wept at these words, but in time they thought of

them no more and made friends with those that were left in the land. They took their wo-men for wives, and their daugh-ters mar-ried their sons. At last some of the chil-dren of Is-ra-el learned to bow down to these gods and the Lord was wroth with them. He sent foes on them who took them and made them slaves. But when they cried to the Lord for help, he pit-ied them and sent men to lead them out to war and make them free. But as soon as they were free they sinned once more. The men who ruled them were called Judg-es.

At one time the king of Mo-ab made war on them. Their judge was named E-hud and he was left hand-ed. He hid a dag-ger and went to the king of Mo-ab's house. And E-hud said, "I have a word from God to speak to thee, O king."

So the rest were sent out and when no one else was there E-hud took out the dag-ger and stab-bed the king so that he fell dead.

Then E-hud fled in haste. But first he locked the doors. No one knew what he had done, and the king's men, when they saw the doors shut, thought that their lord wished to be a-lone. But aft-er a long time they o-pened the doors, and saw that their king was dead.

E-hud went to the land of Ca-naan and blew a trump to call the chil-dren of Is-ra-el. He led them to fight the men of Mo-ab, and the Lord made them win, and the chil-dren of Is-ra-el were set free.

But they sinned once more, and the king of Ca-naan took them and made them his slaves. Then the Lord chose a wo-man to be judge. Her name was Deb-o-rah. She sent for a man called Ba-rak and told him he must go out with troops and fight Sis-e-ra the cap-tain of the king of Ca-naan's men. But he feared to go if Deb-o-rah did not go with him. She said she would go, but he would not have the fame of it for Sis-e-ra would die by the hand of a wo-man.

So Ba-rak took his for-ces and Deb-o-rah went with him. Sis-e-ra brought all the men he could find, but the Lord was not on his side. They fled, and Ba-rak went aft-er them. Sis-e-ra got down out of his char-i-ot and fled on foot.

He came to a tent where a wo-man lived named Ja-el. He did not know she was a friend to the chil-dren of Is-ra-el, and he begged her for a drink. She took a bot-tle of milk and gave him some.

Then he said, "Stand in the door of thy tent and if a-ny one asks if there is a man here, say, 'No.'" So he went in and lay down to sleep.

Then Ja-el took a large nail such as was used to hold down the side of the tent. She went to Sis-e-ra, and drove the nail through his head so that he died.

When Ba-rak came to seek Sis-e-ra, she led him in the tent and showed him the man dead. So the chil-dren of Is-ra-el were set free by the hand of a wo-man as Deb-o-rah had said.

But as soon as they were free they sinned once more, and the Lord let the Mid-i-an-ites take them for slaves. They had to serve them for for-ty years. They drove them out of their homes and they had to live in dens and caves and the grain was kept from them so they had no food.

Now there was a man named Gid-e-on who went to thresh out some wheat one day and tried to hide it from their foes. The Lord came to him in the form of an an-gel, and spoke kind words to him.

Then Gid-e-on told the Lord all the peo-ple had to bear and the Lord said, "Thou shalt set the peo-ple free. I will be with thee, and thy foes shall fall as one man."

Then Gid-e-on said, "Stay, I pray thee, that I may bring thee an of-fer-ing." And he went and killed a kid and brought it to Him. The Lord told him to lay it on a rock, and he did so. Then the Lord touched the flesh with his staff and fire came out of the rock and burnt it up. Then the Lord was no more seen.

So the troops of Mid-i-an came and made their camp in a vale called Jez-reel. Gid-e-on blew his. trump-et to call out the peo-ple to fight them. Then he asked the Lord to give him a sign that He would help him. He said he would lay a fleece of wool on the ground, and let it stay there all night. If it was wet with dew when day came and all the rest of the ground was dry, he would know that the Lord would set them free.

Gid-e-on did as he had said, and when it was light he found that his fleece was so wet that he could wring a bowl of wa-ter out of it, but all the rest of the ground was dry.

Still Gid-e-on wished to try once more, and he begged the Lord to show him by a new way that He meant him

GID-E-ON'S OF-FER-ING IS BURNT BY FIRE FROM THE ROCK.

to lead the peo-ple. He said he would put the fleece out, and leave it all night, and then if it were dry and all the rest of the ground wet he would be sure that the Lord would help him when he went out to fight.

So he left the fleece, and found it in the morn-ing dry, while all the rest of the ground was wet with dew.

Then he rose and took all the for-ces of Is-ra-el and marched on the camp of Mid-i-an.

But the Lord told him not to take all his men, for then if they won they would think it was of their own strength they had done it. He must tell all those who felt the least fear to go back to their homes. Gid-e-on did so and there were ma-ny who left him. But the Lord said there was still too large a force. And he told Gid-e-on to take them down to the wa-ter and He would show him who were to go.

So Gid-e-on led them to the stream. They felt thirst-y and some stooped down and drank, and some lift-ed the wa-ter in their hands. The Lord told Gid-e-on to take all those who drank out of their hands and let the rest go home.

The Mid-i-an-ites had a great force that lay all a-long the val-ley, while Gid-e-on had but three hun-dred men. The Lord told him, if he feared to go with so few, to take a man in the night and go near the camp of the foe so that he might hear what they said. Gid-e-on did so and he heard them tell of their dreams. One said, " I saw in my dream a bar-ley loaf that fell in our camp and struck a tent and threw it down." The man who heard him said, "That bar-ley loaf means the sword of Gid-e-on for the Lord is go-ing to give all our host in-to his hand."

Gid-e-on heard this and called his men to rise and come, for the Lord would help them win the fight. He set them in three parts and gave each man a trump-et and a pitch-er with a light in it. He told them they must watch him and do just as he did when they reached the camp of the foe.

So they got to the camp in the night. And Gid-e-on blew on his trump-et, and broke the pitch-er with a cry, " The sword of the Lord and of Gid-e-on." The rest all did the same, and it made a great noise. The peo-ple of

Mid-i-an were so a-fraid they cried out and fled. They did not know friend from foe in their fright, and killed each oth-er as they ran.

Gid-e-on chased them to the riv-er Jor-dan and took what was left as slaves. So the Is-ra-el-ites were made free.

CHAPTER XVI.

JEPH-THAH'S DAUGH-TER.

BUT in time the Is-ra-el-ites for-got all the Lord had done for them, and when Gid-e-on was dead they turned once more to i-dols. They set up a false god called Ba-al. The son of Gid-e-on, who did not walk in the ways of his fa-ther, went to She-chem and asked the peo-ple there to make him their king. They did so, and gave him much sil-ver, so that he hir-ed bad men to go with him to kill all his broth-ers. But the young-est got a-way.

This bad son's name was A-bim-e-lech and he ruled three years. But God made the peo-ple hate him, so that they laid a plot to kill him. One of the head men was his friend and sent him word of this and told him to hide with his peo-ple in a field so that he could fight those who came a-gainst him He did this, and when the men of She-chem came out he drove them back, and fought all day in the streets of the cit-y, and killed ma-ny.

Then some of the men of She-chem fled to the tem-ple of their i-dol, Ba-al, where no one could reach them.

Then A-bim-e-lech took an axe, and went out and cut down the branch of a tree, and told all his men to do the same. They all piled up the branch-es at the door of the i-dol's house and set fire to them. So it was burned and all the men in it.

Then A-bim-e-lech went to take a town named The-bez. The peo-ple fled to a high tow-er, and he came near the door to set fire to it. But a wo-man threw down a piece of mill-stone and it fell on his head. When he found that he must die, he said to one of his men, "Draw thy sword and slay me, that it be not said I was slain by a wo-man."

The young man drew his sword and thrust it in his breast. So A-bim-e-lech died for his sins.

The chil-dren of Is-ra-el still turned from the true God and bowed down to the false gods of the land. The Lord would not help them and they were once more made slaves.

Then they cried to the Lord for help. But He told them that He had set them free ma-ny times and that they still left Him to serve false gods. Now let them go to those false gods and ask them to help them. But the peo-ple still cried to the Lord, and at last He had pit-y on them.

The Am-mon-ites, whose slaves they were, came out a-gainst them, and the Is-ra-el-ites thought of a brave man named Jeph-thah whom they had treat-ed so bad-ly that he had left his home. Now they sent word for him to come and lead them. But he said, "Did you not hate me? Why then do you call on me now?"

They told him that they want-ed him to lead them to fight the Am-mon-ites, and he should rule all the peo-ple of Gil-e-ad.

So Jeph-thah went with them, and he sent word and asked the king of the Am-mon-ites why he had come to fight them. The king said they had tak-en his land and must give it back.

Jeph-thah sent word to the king that the Lord gave the land to them and they would keep it.

So the Am-mon-ites made read-y to fight, and Jeph-thah led his troops near their camp. And he made a vow to

JEPH-THAH AND HIS DAUGH-TER.

the Lord that if he won the fight he would of-fer up to him as a burnt of-fer-ing what came first out of his door to meet him. This was a wrong vow to make, but as he had made it to the Lord he had to keep it.

So the fight was fought and the Is-ra-el-ites won. Jeph-thah went to his home, and his on-ly child, a fair young girl, came out with great joy to meet him. When he saw her he rent his clothes in great grief, and told her of the vow.

Then she said, "If thou hast made a vow un-to the Lord, do to me as thou hast said."

The Lord did not wish that Jeph-thah should keep such a vow, but he thought he must. So he took his on-ly child and did with her as he had said, and all the young wo-men of Is-ra-el mourned for her.

CHAPTER XVII.

THE STO-RY OF SAM-SON.

ONCE more the chil-dren of Is-ra-el sinned, and were made slaves by the Phil-is-tines.

There was a good man by the name of Ma-no-ah who served the Lord with his wife. The Lord sent an an-gel to the wo-man to tell her that she would have a son who should set his peo-ple free. His hair must not be cut and he must not drink wine, and they must rear him to love and serve God.

Ma-no-ah's wife told him that a man of God had spo-ken to her.   She said, "He had the face of an an-gel, but I did not ask him whence he came."

Then Ma-no-ah prayed, "O Lord, let the man of God whom Thou didst send come to us once more and teach us what we shall do to the child that shall be born."

So the Lord heard him and sent the an-gel to the wo-man as she sat in the field. She made haste and ran and called her hus-band and told him who was there.

So he went with her and asked. "Art thou the man of God who spoke to the wo-man?"   He said. "I am."

And Ma-no-ah asked, "How shall we do with the child?"

And the an-gel said, "Let thy wife do all that I told her be-fore."

Ma-no-ah begged the man to stay and eat food with them, for he did not know he was an an-gel, but he would not.

Then Ma-no-ah took a kid and of-fered it up as a burnt of-fer-ing. and the an-gel went up out of their sight in the flame of the fire.

Then Ma-no-ah said. "We shall die for we have seen God."

But his wife said. "If the Lord meant to kill us He would not have let us of-fer the burnt of-fer-ing. or told us we should have a son."

In due time the babe was born. and they called his name Sam-son.

When he was grown. he loved a daugh-ter of the Phil-is-tines. and wished to make her his wife. But his fa-ther and moth-er did not want him to take her his wife

one who served false gods, and they asked him if he could
not find one in Is-ra-el.   He would not give her up, but
said, "Get her for me, for she pleas-es me well."

So his fa-ther and moth-er went with him to the place
where the maid whom he would wed lived.   As he passed
a place of vines, a young li-on came out and roared at

SAM-SON AND THE LI-ON.

Sam-son.   The Lord gave him strength to kill it with his
hands as if it had been a kid.

Each time he saw the maid he loved her still more, and
at last he went to take her for his wife.

When he reached the spot where he had killed the li-on,

he saw that a swarm of bees had made hon-ey in its dead bod-y. He took some and ate it as he went on, and when he saw his moth-er and fa-ther he gave them some.

Now he made a feast, as was the way when one took a wife in those days. It last-ed sev-en days, and some of the Phil-is-tines were there. Sam-son told them he would give them a rid-dle to guess. If they found it out ere the sev-en days were past, he would give them thir-ty suits of clothes, but if they failed, they must give him thir-ty suits. They said they would and he told them this: "Out of the eat-er came forth meat, and out of the strong came forth sweet-ness." He meant the hon-ey he had found in the li-on. The Phil-is-tines tried three days, and were not pleased that they could not find it out. They went to Sam-son's wife and said they would burn her fa-ther's house, and her too, if she did not help them to find out the rid-dle.

So she coaxed Sam-son, and wept, and said he did not love her. He said he had not told his own fa-ther and moth-er. Still she wept all the time till at last he made it known to her, and she went straight and told her peo-ple.

They made out that they had guessed it, and said, "What is sweet-er than hon-ey, and what is strong-er than a li-on?"

Then Sam-son knew what his wife had done. He went home, but his wife stayed with her peo-ple. God had made him so strong that he might set his peo-ple free.

When the wheat was reaped Sam-son went to see his wife and took her a kid. But her fa-ther would not let him come in the house. He told Sam-son he had giv-en her to be the wife of an-oth-er man.

Then Sam-son was an-gry, and he caught three hun-dred fox-es, and tied bits of light-ed wood to their tails, and let them loose in the fields. The grain was set on fire and the grape vines and ol-ives were burned. The Phil-is-tines found out that it was Sam-son who had done this and they threw his fa-ther and moth-er in the fire. Sam-son fled to the top of a rock called E-tam.

The Phil-is-tines came to take him, and the Is-ra-el-ites feared them.

They went to Sam-son and asked him, "Know-est thou not that the Phil-is-tines rule o-ver us? Why hast thou done these things?"

Sam-son said the Phil-is-tines had done e-vil to him, and so he had done e-vil to them.

Then the men of his own peo-ple told him they had come to bind him and give him up to his foes. Sam-son said they might bind him if they would not kill him.

They told him they would not kill him, but they would bind him fast and give him up to the Phil-is-tines.

So they bound him with two new cords. As they drew near their camp, the foe shout-ed with joy.

Then God gave Sam-son strength to break the cords as if they had been threads burned by fire. And he found the jaw bone of an ass and fought with it, and slew a thou-sand of the Phil-is-tines. When he grew weak the Lord brought wa-ter out of the ground for him, and he drank and grew strong.

At last he came to a town called Ga-za, which was owned by the Phil-is-tines. When they heard he was in the town, they locked the gates and set a guard there, for they meant to kill him as soon as it was day. But Sam-son rose up in the night and took up the gates, posts and all, and put them on his back and left them on the top of a hill.

Now the chief men of the Phil-is-tines longed to find out why Sam-son was so strong, and they went to a friend of his, a wo-man named De-li-lah, and said they would give her a great sum of mon-ey if she could find out. She was not a true friend, so she begged Sam-son to tell her what made him so strong. He did not wish to tell her, but he said if he were bound with sev-en green withes, or slim switch-es from trees, he could not break them.

Now De-li-lah had some Phil-is-tines hid in the house, and they brought her the green withes, and she bound Sam-son with them. When he was bound she cried, "The Phil-is-tines are up-on thee Sam-son." But he broke them as if they had been threads.

Then once more the wo-man begged him to tell her how to bind him. He told her that two new ropes which had not been used would do it. She tried them, but when she called the Phil-is-tines he broke them at once.

Then once more she begged him to tell her and he said if she would braid his long hair in a cer-tain way, the strength would go out of him. But when the Phil-is-tines came he was as strong as be-fore.

Then she told him he had mocked her three times, and

she let him have no rest till at last he told her.   He said
that his hair had not been cut since he was born, but if it
were cut off he would not be more strong than oth-er men.

De-li-lah saw that he spoke the truth.   So she sent for
the Phil-is-tines and told them to bring their gold   So
when Sam-son slept, a man shaved his head.   Then she
cried, " The Phil-is-tines are up-on thee, Sam-son," and he
woke.   He went out to meet them, for he did not know
that his strength was gone, and they took him and bound
him with chains.   Then they put out his eyes so that he

SAM-SON IS CAUGHT AND BOUND BY HIS FOES.

was blind and they shut him up in pris-on and made him grind their corn.

Then Sam-son cried to the Lord, and He had mer-cy on him, and his hair grew and his strength came back to him.

One day the Phil-is-tines made a feast to Da-gon, their God, and they said, " Send for Sam-son that he may make sport for us."

So the poor blind man was brought and set down by the posts of the house of their i-dol. He was led there by a boy, for he could not see how to go. Now the house was full of peo-ple, and there were ma-ny on the roof. Sam-son asked the boy to let him feel the posts that he might lean on them. Then he prayed to God and said, " O Lord, give me strength once more," and he put each arm round a post. He said, " Let me die with the Phil-is-tines," and he bowed down with all his might, till the posts moved, and the house fell, and all were killed. Sam-son died too, but he had slain more of the foe in his death than he had done in all his life.

The chil-dren of Is-ra-el took the dead bod-y and laid him with his fa-ther.

CHAPTER XVIII.

THE STO-RY OF RUTH.

THERE was a man of the chil-dren of Is-ra-el who had gone to live in Mo-ab for a while. He had a wife and two sons. The man died and his sons took wives in

Mo-ab. Then, in ten years, they died too. So the moth-er wished to go back to her own land.

When her sons' wives heard this they wept. One of them, named Or-pah, kissed her and went to her own home, but Ruth said she would not leave her. "Where thou go-est I will go, and where thou liv-est I will live. Thy peo-ple shall be my peo-ple, and thy God my God. Where thou di-est I will die, and there will I be bur-ied."

When Na-o-mi saw how Ruth loved her she let her go with her to the land of Ca-naan. They reached Na-o-mi's old home at the time when the fields of bar-ley were ripe.

And Na-o-mi found one of her kin, a rich man named Bo-az, who had great fields of grain. Ruth said, "Let me go out in the fields and glean ears of corn." The Lord had said those who reaped must leave some for the poor, who could pick up what was left. This was what it meant to glean. Now Na-o-mi was poor, so she gave Ruth leave to go and glean.

Now she was in one of the fields of Bo-az when he came to look at the men's work. He saw Ruth and asked, "Who is this?" They told him that she had come with Na-o-mi out of Mo-ab.

Then Bo-az spoke some kind words to Ruth. He told her she could glean in all his fields and need go no where else. When she thirst-ed, his young men would draw wa-ter for her. Ruth bowed down to the ground and asked Bo-az why he was so kind. He said he had heard how she had left her own land and home and friends to stay with Na-o-mi and that God would re-ward her.

RUTH AND BO-AZ

And he told her that she might eat and drink with his peo-ple at meal time, and she did so. And Bo-az told his young men to let fall some ears of corn for her, and some bar-ley. So she gleaned in the field till it was night, and then beat out the grain she had gleaned and took it home.

When Na-o-mi saw how much she had brought she was glad, and asked who the man was who had been so kind to her. Ruth said his name was Bo-az. Then Na-o-mi knew that he was near kin to her, and she told Ruth to do all that he said. So Ruth went to glean till the grain was all reaped.

Then Na-o-mi said that Bo-az meant to thresh out the

grain that night, and Ruth must go and say to him the words she would tell her.

So Ruth went, and Bo-az threshed his bar-ley and then had a feast. Then Ruth came to him and spoke and told him he was their near-est kin, and begged him to be kind to her.

He told her not to fear, he would give her all she need-ed, for he knew she was a good wo-man. And he said, " Bring here thy veil and hold it out," and he poured in it six meas-ures of bar-ley. Ruth took it to Na-o-mi and she told her to wait and see what Bo-az would do.

It was the way in those days that when a man had made up his mind to do a thing, he sat down in the gates of the cit-y and spoke of it to the chief men. So the next day Bo-az told them he meant to take Ruth for his wife. Then they prayed that the Lord would bless Ruth and Bo-az. Na-o-mi was glad of this good news. When Ruth was the wife of Bo-az, and a son was born, she took the lit-tle ba-by and nursed it for them. The child was named O-bed.

CHAPTER XIX.

THE STO-RY OF SAM-U-EL.

THERE was a wo-man in the cit-y of Ra-mah who went up each year to the ark at Shi-loh to pray. She had no child and she asked the Lord to give her a son. She made a vow to God that if He would grant her wish, she

would bring up her son to be the Lord's. Now E-li was
high priest in those days, and he saw how she prayed and
wept. He asked her the cause, and she told him she
sought help from the Lord. He said, "Go in peace and
may God give thee the wish of thy heart."

So she was glad and went to her own home. In time
the Lord sent her a son, and she called him Sam-u-el.
She wait-ed till he was old e-nough, and then she took
him to E-li and said; "O my Lord. For this child I
prayed and the Lord gave me what I asked, so I give
him back to the Lord." And she left him to serve E-li
in the house of the Lord.

THE MOTH-ER OF SAM-U-EL BRINGS HIM TO E-LI.

Now E-li had two sons who were priests, but they were not good men. They took more than their share of the gifts brought to the Lord.

But Sam-u-el did right and the Lord loved him. Each year his par-ents came there to pray, and E-li said God would bless them, in that they had giv-en their son to the Lord.

Now E-li was old, and he heard with grief of the wrong his sons did, but he let them be priests still. Then God was wroth with E-li, and said he should not be priest a-ny more and that both of his sons should die on the same day.

Sam-u-el stayed on to serve him, and one night when he had lain down to sleep he heard a voice that called him. He said, "Here am I" and ran to E-li. Then E-li knew it was the Lord who had called the child, and he said, "Go lie down and if the voice call thee, say, 'Speak Lord for thy serv-ant hear-eth.'" Sam-u-el did so, and then the Lord told to him what he meant to do to E-li and his sons.

Sam-u-el rose up when it was day, but he feared to tell E-li the sad news. E-li called him and asked, "What is the thing the Lord hath said un-to thee? Hide it not from me." Then Sam-u-el told him all.

When E-li heard it he said, "It is the Lord, let Him do what seem-eth Him good."

The words of the Lord came true. The peo-ple went to fight the Phil-is-tines, and they thought they would win if they took the ark of the Lord with them. So the two sons of E-li bore the ark. But the Lord taught them they must trust in Him and in noth-ing else. So the Phil-is-tines fought them, and slew ma-ny, and took the ark.

The two sons of E-li were killed. A man ran from the ar-my to tell the bad news. E-li sat by the road side to hear of the fight. When the man told those in the cit-y, they all cried out with fear. Now E-li was old, and his sight was dim, but he heard the cries and he said, "What means this noise?"

Then the man ran to him and said, "I have come to day from the ar-my. The men of Is-ra-el have fled from the Phil-is-tines and ma-ny are slain. Thy two sons are dead and the ark of God is tak-en."

When E-li heard this his grief was so great that he fell from his seat and his neck broke. So he died.

The Phil-is-tines took the ark with them, but the Lord sent sick-ness to them, so that they were a-fraid and called their wise men to know how they should send it back. These men told the Phil-is-tines to take two cows, and put them to a cart, and lay the ark on it. Then they must let the cows draw it where they chose. If they went to the camp of Is-ra-el it would show that the Lord had meant them to send it back. But if the cows did not take the ark there, then they would know that all their woes had come just by chance.

So the Phil-is-tines did as the wise men said, and as soon as the cows were loose they went straight to the camp of Is-ra-el. There was great joy when the chil-dren of Is-ra-el first saw it.

The cows stopped in a field by a great stone that was there, and some men of the tribe of Le-vi took the ark down and set it on this stone. They broke the cart, and burnt the wood and of-fered up the cows to the Lord.

Now E-li was dead and Sam-u-el was made judge The peo-ple sinned once more and bowed down to strange gods. Then the Phil-is-tines made war on them but Sam-u-el led them to a place called Miz-peh, and prayed, and the Lord heard him and sent a storm so that their foes fled. Sam-u-el set up a stone in that place and called it Eb-en-e-zer, which means, "The stone of help."

Sam-u-el grew old, and he made his two sons judg-es to help him. But they did not do right, for they took bribes, or gifts, and would let men do wrong if they paid them for it.

The chief men of Is-ra-el came to Sam-u-el and told him what his sons had done. They said he must choose them a king. Now the Lord was their king and it was wrong for them to ask such a thing. Sam-u-el prayed to the Lord to know what he should do.

The Lord told him to tell the peo-ple that if they had a king he would take their sons to work for him in the fields, and their daugh-ters to serve him. He would take the best of all they had, and they would cry out to the Lord in that day, but the Lord would not hear them.

Sam-u-el told them all this, but they still said, "We will have a king, that he may rule us and lead us to war like the rest of the na-tions."

So the Lord told Sam-u-el to choose them a king.

Now there was à young man named Saul who was tall and well formed and hand-some. He had gone out to look for some ass-es that his fa-ther had lost. But as they could not be found he turned back to go home. When he reached a cit-y of that land, a man told him there was a proph-et there named Sam-u-el whose word al-ways came true. He said, "Let us go and ask him; he may tell us of the ass-es."

Now it was a feast day in that town, and when they went in, Sam-u-el met them.

The Lord had told Sam-u-el that he would send him a man that day to be king of Is-ra-el. When he met Saul, the Lord said to him, "This is the man."

Saul did not know Sam-u-el, and he asked him where the proph-et lived.

Sam-u-el said, "I am the proph-et" and he bade him come to his house with his serv-ant. He said Saul need not think of the ass-es, for his fa-ther had found them.

So Sam-u-el gave Saul the best place at the feast, and he stayed there all that day. The next day at dawn Sam-u-el took Saul to the top of the house and talked with him. Then he went part of the way with him to the gate of the cit-y.

It was the way in those days that when one was made king oil was poured on the head. So Sam-u-el poured oil on Saul's head, and he was made king, but the chil-dren of Is-ra-el did not know it till they were called to meet at Miz-peh. Then he hid from them at first, but when he was brought out they saw how tall he was, and Sam-u-el

said, "See the man whom the Lord hath chos-en, there
is none like him." Then they all shout-ed, "God save
the king."

Now in one part of the land the Is-ra-el-ites had to
fight with the Am-mon-ites, and they feared them. These
peo-ple want-ed to make slaves of them and said they
would put out their eyes. So the chil-dren of Is-ra-el sent
to Gib-e-ah, where Saul lived, and told of their sad plight,
and the peo-ple wept to hear it. Saul came in just then
with a herd of cat-tle, and he asked, "Why do the peo-
ple weep?" They told him and he took two ox-en and cut
them up and sent the pie-ces all through the land with the
word that "who-ev-er does not come to fight the Am-mon-
ites, the same shall be done to his ox-en." So great crowds
came, and Saul led them, and their foes were put to flight.

Sam-u-el had grown old by this time, and he spoke
to the peo-ple and said that they had sinned in that they
want-ed a king when the Lord was their king, and they
would see what the Lord would do to them.

Now it was the time of wheat har-vest, and he called to
the Lord to send a storm, that they might know that He
was not pleased with them. So a great rain fell all that
day on the ripe wheat, and the peo-ple all feared the Lord
and begged Sam-u-el to pray that they might not be put
to death.

Sam-u-el told them not to fear. Though they had sinned, if they now would serve the Lord He would take
care of them. But if they went aft-er strange gods they
would per-ish.

CHAPTER XX.

THE Phil-is-tines rose up in their might when Saul had been. king for two years. When the Is-ra-el-ites saw so great a host they hid in caves and pits in the earth. Some few stayed with Saul, their king, and he led them to Gil-gal. Sam-u-el had said he would meet him there, and tell him what to do. But he did not come in sev-en days, and so Saul made a burnt of-fer-ing to the Lord. Sam-u-el came then and told Saul that he had done wrong, and that the Lord would not let him be king, but would choose a new man.

Now the Is-ra-el-ites had been slaves to the Phil-is-tines for a long time, and there were no smiths in the land, for the Phil-is-tines feared that if they let a-ny stay there they would make for the peo-ple swords and spears, with which to fight. And so it was that a-mong all the Is-ra-el-ites none had a sword or a spear but Saul and his son Jon-a-than.

In those times the men who fought bore shields made of wood with brass or i-ron on them, and kings and chiefs had young men to hold their shields and spears when they were not in use. These men were called ar-mor bear-ers.

One day Jon-a-than called his ar-mor bear-er, and asked him to go with him to the camp of the Phil-is-tines, for who knew what the Lord might do for them. The young man said he would go. Jon-a-than said this would be the

way they might tell if the Lord would help them. They
would go and stand where the Phil-is-tines could see them,
and if the foe called out to them and told them to wait
they would take it for a sign that the Lord would not
help them. But if the foe said, "Come up to us," they
would know that God would make them win.

So they did so, and the Phil-is-tines said, "See, they are
com-ing out of their holes," and they called out, "Come up
to us and we will show you some-thing." So Jon-a-than
and his man climbed up the rocks and fought with the foe
and killed twen-ty of them. God made the earth to heave
so that the Phil-is-tines were in great fear.

Now Saul did not know of this, but the guard looked
out at the camp of the Phil-is-tines and saw that there was
a fight there. They told Saul, and he count-ed his men and
found that he missed Jon-a-than and his ar-mor bear-er.
Then he took his men and went and joined in the fight,
and those who were hid in caves and pits came out, and
none tast-ed food that day. For Saul had said they must
not take time to eat, but chase the foe while it was light.

Now Jon-a-than did not know of this, so when they
came to a place where the wild bees had made a nest in
the trees and hon-ey dropped from it, he dipped the end
of his staff in it and ate. Saul heard of this, and he was
wroth, and said Jon-a-than must die. But the peo-ple cried
out for him, and saved him, for they said he had caused
them to put their foes to rout.

Then the Lord sent the Is-ra-el-ites to fight the Am-a-
lek-ites, and put them to death with all their flocks and

herds. But Saul saved the best of the cat-tle a-live, and the Lord was not pleased, as he did not o-bey Him.

Sam-u-el came and asked Saul a-bout it. But Saul said he had done as the Lord bade him. At the same time Sam-u-èl heard the sheep bleat and the ox-en low. He asked Saul what this meant. Saul said the peo-ple had kept these to of-fer up to the Lord. Sam-u-el said, " It was bet-ter to o-bey than to of-fer up sac-ri-fi-ces." Then he told Saul once more that the Lord would not let him be king, but would put a man in his place.

The Lord told Sam-u-el to go to Beth-le-hem to a man

SAM-U-EL A-NOINTS DA-VID.

named Jes-se, and take one of his sons for a king. But Sam-u-el feared that Saul would kill him. Then the Lord told him to go and make a burnt of-fer-ing there and ask Jes-se to come. Sam-u-el did so, and Jes-se came with his sons. They all passed in his sight, and he asked, "Are these all?" Jes-se said, "There is one left who tends the sheep; he is the young-est." So Sam-u-el said, "Send for him." When he came he was fair to see and his cheeks were red. The Lord said to Sam-u-el, "A-noint him, for this is he." So the Lord chose Da-vid to be king and made him good and wise.

Now Saul did not know of these things, but he was not at ease in his mind. He could not sleep, and he sent out to look for a man who could play the harp well, for he thought that might soothe him. It chanced that Da-vid was brought to play for him. He came and wait-ed on Saul and played for him and pleased him. He stayed there till Saul grew bet-ter and then he went back to his own home.

Once more the Phil-is-tines brought a great host to fight Is-ra-el. Each na-tion pitched its camp on a mount-ain. There was a gi-ant with the Phil-is-tines named Go-li-ath of Gath. He wore a coat of brass and a helm-et on his head. He came out where all could see him and cried out, "Choose a man and let him come and fight me. If he kill me we will be your slaves, but if I kill him you shall be my slaves!"

Now the gi-ant was so great that no one was found to go out and fight him, and Saul was in great fear. Just

DA-VID AND SAUL.

then Da-vid came to the camp to bring his three broth-ers some loaves of bread and corn, and to see how they were. He came just as the two ar-mies were go-ing to fight. For the Is-ra-el-ites had no man to meet the gi-ant, and they had to fight as best they could.

Now while Da-vid talked with his broth-ers, the gi-ant came out once more and said the same words. If there was a man who could kill him, Saul said he would give him great rich-es and the king's daugh-ter should be his wife. Da-vid asked all a-bout it. E-li-ab, his eld-est broth-er, sneered and asked, "What brought you here, and where have you left those few sheep? You want to see the fight?"

But Da-vid said, "What harm have I done to thee?
Who is this Phil-is-tine that he should de-fy the ar-mies
of the liv-ing God?" Some who heard these words told
them to Saul and he sent for Da-vid.

Da-vid said, "Let no man's heart be a-fraid. I will go
and fight this Phil-is-tine."

Saul said, "Thou art not a-ble, for thou art but a youth
and he hath been a man of war from his youth."

But Da-vid told how he had killed a li-on and bear, and
saved a lamb of his flock, and he thought the Lord would
help him. So Saul said, "Go and the Lord be with thee."
And he gave him his own ar-mor, and his coat of mail
and sword. But Da-vid said, "I can-not go with these,"
and he put them off. He took his staff and chose five
smooth stones from the brook, and he took his sling in his
hand. When he came near the Phil-is-tines' ranks, the
gi-ant scorned him, for he looked like a boy. Go-li-ath
said, "Am I a dog that thou com-est with a staff to me?"
And he called on his false gods to curse Da-vid, and told
him to come near that he might kill him.

Then Da-vid said, "Thou com-est to me trust-ing in thy
sword and spear. But I come to thee trust-ing in the God
of Is-ra-el. For this day, He will give thee in-to my hand
and I will kill thee, and cut off thy head from thee, and
the Phil-is-tines shall be slain and their dead bod-ies shall
lie on the ground and the birds of the air and the wild
beasts of the field shall eat them.

Then as Go-li-ath came on, Da-vid ran and took a stone
out of his bag and slung it. It struck the gi-ant in the

DA-VID SLAYS GO-LI-ATH.

head with such force that it sank in and he fell. Then
Da-vid took the gi-ant's sword from him and cut off his
great head. When the Phil-is-tines saw this they fled, but
the troops of Is-ra-el shouted and gave chase to them, and
ma-ny fell by the way. All the gold and sil-ver and rich
robes fell in-to the hands of the Is-ra-el-ites.

Then Da-vid was brought to Saul, with the head of
Go-li-ath in his hand. Saul asked him whose son he was,
and Da-vid said, "I am the son of thy serv-ant, Jes-se,
the Beth-le-hem-ite."

Now Jon-a-than saw Da-vid and loved him as his own soul, and they were friends from that day. Saul kept Da-vid with him, and to show his love he took off the robe he wore and put it on Da-vid and gave him his sword and bow.

But once when they had won a fight with the Phil-is-tines, and the wo-men came with song and dance to meet them, they praised Da-vid more than Saul. From that time Saul was not pleased, and the next time Da-vid played on the harp for him he tried to kill him with a spear. · But Da-vid stepped one side and his life was saved. Then Saul feared Da-vid, and sent him off with his troop. The Lord helped him and the peo-ple loved him. Saul sent him to fight the Phil-is-tines in the hope that they would kill him. He told Da-vid that if he won he would give him Me-rab, his daugh-ter, for his wife. Da-vid fought well, but Saul did not keep his word. He gave Me-rab to an-oth-er. Then his daugh-ter Mi-chal loved Da-vid, and Saul found it out. He said that if Da-vid would kill a hun-dred Phil-is-tines he should have her for his wife. Da-vid did so, and this time Saul had to keep his word, but he hat-ed him still more. He laid plots to kill him, but Jon-a-than told Da-vid of them and begged him to go and hide. He said he would talk to his fa-ther.

Jon-a-than plead-ed for Da-vid and told of all he had done, how he had saved Is-ra-el. Saul knew it all and at last he said Da-vid's life should be safe. So Jon-a-than told Da-vid and he came back to live in Saul's house once more and fought with the Phil-is-tines and gained the fight. Saul saw that the peo-ple loved Da-vid more than they did him, and he tried once more to kill him. Da-vid fled that night.

Saul sent men to his house to take him, but Da-vid's wife let him down through a win-dow. Then she made up an im-age and laid it in his bed, so that he should have time to get off. They thought he slept, but when they went to take him they found him not, and Saul was wroth.

Da-vid went to his friend Sam-u-el and told him all. Saul tried to take him but the Lord saved him.

Then Da-vid went to Jon-a-than and asked, " What is my sin that thy fa-ther seek-eth to kill me?"

Jon-a-than said, "Thou shalt not die," and he said he would do for Da-vid all he asked.

Now there was to be a feast the next day at Saul's house, but Da-vid feared to go. He wished to stay a-way three days, and he told Jon-a-than to say to Saul if he asked for him that he had gone home to see his own peo-ple and to of-fer up the year-ly sac-ri-fice. If Saul was an-gry it would show he meant him harm.

Jon-a-than told him he would do so, and at the end of the three days he must come and hide by a rock in the field there. He would come out with a lad and shoot at a mark. If he said when the lad went to pick the ar-rows up, "The ar-rows are on this side," then Da-vid would know that Saul would not harm him. But if he said to the boy, "The ar-rows are be-yond," then Da-vid must fly for his life.

Saul did not ask for Da-vid on the first day of the feast, but on the sec-ond day he said, "Why comes not Da-vid to eat?"

Jon-a-than told him, and he was ver-y an-gry. He told Jon-a-than he would not be king when he should die if Da-vid were not put to death. When his son plead-ed for Da-vid he cast a spear at him. Then Jon-a-than would not eat, but went out and was grieved for Da-vid.

On the third day he went as he had said with the boy. When he shot an ar-row that passed by the lad he cried, "The ar-row is be-yond thee—make haste," Da-vid knew then that Saul meant to kill him and he must fly.

Jon-a-than sent off the lad and Da-vid came out and bowed down to the ground three times. But Jon-a-than kissed him and they both wept. They loved each oth-er so much that they vowed they would be kind to each oth-er al-ways and to each oth-er's chil-dren. So Da-vid fled, and Jon-a-than went back home.

Now Da-vid went to a place called Nob where the ark of God was. But when the high priest sent to ask why he had come, he feared to tell the truth and said he was sent by the king.

This was wrong in Da-vid, for he should have trust-ed in God. There were some young men who had joined Da-vid, and he asked that they should have five loaves of bread. The priest said he had no bread but that which was left on the gold-en ta-ble in the Lord's house. This was called shew-bread. So he gave that to Da-vid. Then he asked the high priest for a sword or spear. There

DA-VID AND JON-A-THAN.

was noth-ing there but the sword of Go-li-ath of Gath, whom Da-vid had slain, and the priest gave that to him.

Then Da-vid went and hid in a cave. His broth-ers heard of it and came to him, and more friends joined him there. He asked the king of Mo-ab to let his fa-ther and moth-er live in that land till he should see what the Lord would do for him. He used to think of the days of his youth while he lived in that cave, and of the well by the gate where the wa-ter had tast-ed so sweet to him. Once he said, "Oh that some one would give me a drink from the well by the gate at Beth-le-hem." Three of his men loved him so much that they broke through the camp of the Phil-is-tines and got some of the wa-ter. But when Da-vid knew they had risked their lives for it, he would not drink it.

Then there was a proph-et who came to Da-vid and told him to go out of the cave and go back to the land of Ju-dah.

Saul was there, and one told him how the high priest had giv-en Da-vid the sword of Go-li-ath and the shew-bread. Saul sent for that high priest and asked him why he had done this and helped Da-vid rise up a-gainst him. The high priest said he did not know that Da-vid had fled from Saul. Saul was ver-y an-gry and told his men to slay the high priest and all his fam-i-ly. But the men feared to do so. Then he found one bad man who would do it and he went to the high priest's home and slew him and all there, but one son. This son's name was A-bi-a-thar, and he went to Da-vid and told him all. Da-vid kept him with him and said no one should harm him.

Then Da-vid heard that the Phil-is-tines were at Kei-lah, and he asked the Lord what he should do. The Lord told him to go and fight them and save the place. He did so and saved Kei-lah.

Saul heard of this and thought that now he could take Da-vid. He called his troops and Da-vid heard of it. He asked the Lord if Saul would come to Kei-lah. The Lord said, " He will sure-ly come." Then Da-vid asked if the peo-ple would fight for him or if they would give him up. And the Lord said, "They will give thee up."

So Da-vid fled and hid in a wood. Jon-a-than went to

see him there, and spoke kind words to him. He said,
" Fear not! Saul will not find thee, and thou shalt yet be
king of Is-ra-el." And they vowed once more to be strong
friends.

Each time Saul tried to harm Da-vid, the Lord saved
him. Once Saul went in-to the ver-y cave where Da-vid
was hid-den. It was dark there, and Da-vid might have
killed Saul, but he would not. He went up ver-y soft-ly
and cut off a piece of his robe, but Saul did not know it.

When Saul went out, Da-vid came forth and cried,
" My Lord, the king." Saul turned and Da-vid fell on
his face. Then he asked Saul why he wished to kill him
when he had done no wrong. He said he had the chance
to kill Saul that day and his men begged him to do it, but
he would not harm his king. Then Da-vid showed the
piece of the robe he had cut off, so that Saul could see
how near to him he had been.

When Saul heard Da-vid's kind words his heart melt-ed
and he said, "Is this thy voice, my son Da-vid ? " and
he wept.

Then he said, "Thou hast done good when I have done
e-vil. The Lord re-ward thee. I know well that thou
shalt one day be king o-ver Is-ra-el." And he asked
Da-vid to prom-ise that when he was king he would not
slay his chil-dren. Da-vid said he would not, and Saul
went to his home.

Sam-u-el died and all Is-ra-el mourned for him. Then
Da-vid went to Pa-ran to live. There was a rich man
named Na-bal there, who had a good and fair wife named

Ab-i-gail. He was a bad man, and he had his flocks feed-ing near where Da-vid was. When Na-bal went to shear his sheep, Da-vid sent some of his young men to see if they could get some food from him. But Na-bal asked, "Who is Da-vid? There are plen-ty of men who have run a-way from their mas-ters as he has done."

When the young men told Da-vid he said, "Gird on your swords." Da-vid too put on his sword, for he was an-gry. He said he had kept Na-bal's flocks safe and not one was lost, and now he would not give them food.

There was a young man who told Na-bal's wife how good Da-vid had been to them, and how he and his men had guard-ed Na-bal's flocks in the des-ert, and how they had been treat-ed.

So Ab-i-gail made haste and took loaves of bread, and sheep, and parched corn, and wine, and figs, and rais-ins, and load-ed them on the ass-es and went out to meet Da-vid.

When she saw him and his men she bowed down to him, and begged him to take what she had brought. She said she knew the Lord would bless him and make him king, and then he would be glad he had heard her and not killed Na-bal.

Da-vid took the gifts she had brought and spoke kind words to her, and thanked the Lord He had kept him from kill-ing Na-bal in his an-ger.

When Ab-i-gail reached home there was a feast there, and Na-bal had drank so much wine that she did not tell him then how she had saved his life. When he did hear

it, he was in such fear that his strength all went from him
and in ten days he died.

When Da-vid heard this he said, "Bless-ed be the Lord
who has kept me from e-vil." And he loved Ab-i-gail,
and took her for his wife.

CHAPTER XXI.

THE DEATH OF SAUL.

Now Saul still hat-ed Da-vid in his heart and want-ed
to kill him. So when he heard where he was, he went
out with some men to find him. Da-vid sent some spies
to watch, and they brought back word that Saul was come.

Then Da-vid called his neph-ew, and in the night they
went down to Saul's camp. Saul slept with his spear
stuck in the ground near him. Da-vid's neph-ew wished
to strike the spear through Saul, but Da-vid would not let
him, for he would not strike one whom God had made king.

But Da-vid said they would take the spear and cruse of
wa-ter and go. No one saw what they did, and Saul was
in a deep sleep.

Then Da-vid went to the top of a hill and cried out to
Saul's men. Saul's cap-tain, Ab-ner, waked up and asked,
"Who art thou that cri-est out?"

Da-vid said, "Why keep ye not bet-ter watch of the
king? See where his spear is, and the cruse of wa-ter."

Saul heard Da-vid and he asked, "Is that thy voice, my

son Da-vid?" Then once more Da-vid asked how he had done him a-ny harm, and showed him how he might have killed him but would not.

And Saul said, "I have sinned! Come back, my son Da-vid, and I will not harm thee."

And Da-vid showed him the spear and asked him to send one of his young men for it. Then Saul said he would go back to his own home.

But Da-vid did not trust him, for he had said all this be-fore, so he thought it would be best for him to go with his men in-to the land of the Phil-is-tines. He did so, and the peo-ple of that land let them stay there, for they hoped

DA-VID SPARES SAUL'S LIFE.

to make slaves of them. When they had been there some
time, the Phil-is-tines went out to fight Saul.

Now when Saul saw the host that had come to fight
him, he asked the Lord what he should do. But the Lord
would not tell him. He was at his wits' end. So he
sought out a wo-man who was called a witch and went to
her at night to ask her if she could bring back the dead.

She asked, "Whom shall I bring up?"

He said, "Bring up Sam-u-el."

Then Sam-u-el seemed to come to him, and Saul bowed
to the ground.

Sam-u-el asked, "Why hast thou brought me?" Saul
said, "I am in great grief, for God has left me, and I have
called thee to know what I shall do."

Sam-u-el said, "The Lord has done as I told thee He
would do. He has put thee from be-ing king, and made
Da-vid king, be-cause thou hast not served him. He will
make the Phil-is-tines win in the fight, and on the mor-row
thou and thy sons shall be with me a-mong the dead."

And Saul fell on his face and all his strength left him.
He had not tast-ed food that day. The wo-man begged
him to eat. At first he would not, but at last he ate of
the food she brought.

When the Phil-is-tines went out to fight they took
Da-vid and his men with them. But some said this would
not be safe, for Da-vid might turn and fight on the side
of Is-ra-el. So they were sent back. When they reached
their homes they found all their hous-es had been burned
and their wives and chil-dren car-ried off for slaves by

THE WITCH BRINGS UP SAM-U-EL.

the Am-a-lek-ites. Then the Is-ra-el-ites were an-gry with Da-vid and want-ed to stone him, but the Lord took care of him.

Then Da-vid asked A-bi-a-thar, the high priest, to speak to the Lord and see if it was His will that he should go and fight the Am-a-lek-ites. The Lord said, "Go, and thou shalt get back all they have tak-en." So Da-vid went, and in one place they found a young man sick and faint. They gave him food, for he had not eat-en in three days. Then they asked him where he was from, and he said he had served an Am-a-lek-ite and had been left when he fell

sick. He told Da-vid how they had burnt Zik-lag with
fire. Da-vid asked him to take him to the camp of the
foe. He said he would do so if they would not kill him
or let him be tak-en. Da-vid told him he should be safe,
so he brought them to the place. The Am-a-lek-ites had
a feast and there and then Da-vid with his men fell on
them and slew them, so that none got a-way but some
of the young men who fled on cam-els. Then the Is-ra-
el-ites got back all the spoil that the foe had tak-en, and
their flocks and herds also.

Now the Phil-is-tines had gone out to fight Saul and his
men, and they won, and slew Jon-a-than and two more of
Saul's sons. Saul too was so wound-ed that he said to his
ar-mor-bear-er, " Draw thy sword and put me to death
lest I fall in the hands of the Phil-is-tines." But the man
was a-fraid. Then Saul took his own sword and set it on
the ground so that the point was up and fell on it, so that
it killed him.

The ar-mor-bear-er saw that Saul was dead and it scared
him so much that he fell on his own sword and died too.
So the Phil-is-tines won, and all had come to pass as
Sam-u-el had told to Saul. The Is-ra-el-ites fled, and the
Phil-is-tines cut off the head of Saul, and placed the dead
bod-ies of him and his sons on the wall of Beth-shan.
But the Is-ra-el-ites, when they heard this, rose and went
to the place, and took down the bod-ies, and burnt them,
and laid their ash-es in a grave un-der a tree in Ja-besh.

CHAPTER XXII.

When Da-vid heard the sad news that the Is-ra-el-ites had fled from the Phil-is-tines, and that Saul and Jon-a-than were dead, his grief was ver-y great. The young man who brought the news told him that Saul had asked him to kill him, for he was sore wound-ed; and he said he had done so. He knew Saul was no friend to Da-vid, and he hoped to get some gift for this news. But Da-vid rent his clothes, and he and his men wept for Saul and Jon-a-than, and for all who had been slain. And Da-vid said the young man must die for his sin, for he had said he had killed the King of Is-ra-el. Then Da-vid asked the Lord if he should go back to the land of Is-ra-el.

The Lord told him to go to the cit-y of He-bron. He did so, and the men of Ju-dah came there and made him their king. But the rest of the tribes did not come, for one of Saul's sons ruled them. But one day two men killed him and took his head to Da-vid. They thought this would please him, but he said they must die for their sin.

From that time Da-vid was king of all the tribes. He went to Je-ru-sa-lem and took a strong fort that was on Mount Zi-on and lived in it. He grew rich and great. He took men with him to bring the ark of God back from the house where it had been left so long. In this

THE DEATH OF SAUL.

time the peo-ple had for-got to care for the ark, where once God had come in a cloud to speak to them. They for-got that no one was to touch it but the priests and Le-vites. So when the ox-en that drew it stum-bled, Uz-zah, who helped drive the cart, put his hand on the ark, and dropped down dead. Da-vid was an-gry that the Lord had killed Uz-zah. He would not take the ark on, but left it in the house of a Le-vite, where it stayed three months.

The Lord blessed all those that were in that house while it was there.

When Da-vid heard this he sent for the ark, and it was borne by Le-vites with great joy to the tent he had built for it in Je-ru-sa-lem. But as Da-vid sat in his grand house he thought he would like to build a house for the ark of the Lord. He asked the proph-et Na-than if he should do this, but the Lord told Na-than that the son of Da-vid should build the house.

Now when Da-vid had grown rich and great he thought of the vow he had made with Jon-a-than. He sent to see if there were a-ny of Jon-a-than's chil-dren left, so that he might be kind to them. He found there was one son. He had been a child on the day his fa-ther was killed, and the nurse had picked him up and fled. But she had let him fall, and he had been lame since that day. He was named Me-phib-o-sheth, and was then a man.

Da-vid sent for him, and he came and bowed down to the ground. Da-vid told him not to fear. He said, " I will be kind to thee for thy fa-ther's sake, and thou shalt have all the land of Saul, and thou shalt come and eat at my ta-ble." And it was so.

Now Da-vid did e-vil in the sight of the Lord. He was on the roof of his house one day, and he saw a fair wo-man. He found out that she was the wife of a man named U-ri-ah. He sent U-ri-ah to the bat-tle field, with word that he must be put in front in the thick of the fight. He said they must then fly and leave him there. He wished him slain so that he might take his wife for his own. Jo-ab, his cap-tain, did as he said. He put U-ri-ah in front, where he was killed, and sent word of it to Da-vid. Then the king brought Bath-she-ba, the wife of U-ri-ah, to his house and made her his wife.

The Lord was wroth with Da-vid, and sent Na-than the proph-et to him. And Na-than said to Da-vid, "There were two men in one cit-y. One was rich, and one was poor. The rich man had great flocks and herds, but the poor man had on-ly one lamb. He had fed it, and it slept in his bo-som. Now there came a guest to the house of the rich man, and he would not take one of his own flock, though he had so ma-ny, but he took the poor man's lamb and killed it so that his friend might eat."

When Da-vid heard this he said, "The man who has done this shall sure-ly be put to death, and he shall give back to the poor man four times as much as he took from him."

And Na-than said un-to Da-vid, "Thou art the man!" And he told him how rich and great God had made him, yet he had caused a man to be put to death that he might take his wife. And Na-than said the Lord would bring great grief on him for his sin.

Now God gave a son to Da-vid and Bath-she-ba, and they loved him ver-y much. But he grew ver-y sick. Da-vid fast-ed and prayed that he might not die. He would not taste food, his grief was so great. On the sev-enth day the child died. Then Da-vid's men feared to tell him But he asked them, "Is the child dead?" They said, "He is dead."

Then Da-vid rose up, and washed and dressed, and went to the tent where the ark was kept, and prayed to God, and when he came back he sat down and ate food. His men said it was strange that while the child was sick he would not eat, but now it was dead he could take food. Da-vid said, "While the child lived I fast-ed and wept, for I said, 'Who can tell wheth-er God will be kind to me and let the child live?' But now he is dead, why should I fast a-ny more? Can I bring him back to me? I shall go to him when I die, but he shall nev-er re-turn un-to me."

God gave a son to Bath-she-ba and Da-vid, and they called him Sol-o-mon, which means Peace-a-ble.

Da-vid had oth-er sons too. One of them, named Ab-sa-lom, was ver-y hand-some, and praised through all the land for his good looks. His hair was ver-y thick and long, and he was well formed. But his heart was bad, for he killed his broth-er Am-non and had to flee from the land. At the end of three years he came back, but Da-vid would not see him or speak to him.

At last Ab-sa-lom got Jo-ab to speak to the king for him, and Da-vid let him come to see him. When Ab-sa-lom bowed down to him, he raised him and kissed him, for he loved him. Then Ab-sa-lom put on great state, and had men to run in front of his char-i-ot when he rode out, and he talked of the great things he would do if he were king, and how each man's wrongs should be right-ed. So he made ma-ny trust him.

When he thought it safe he went to Da-vid and said,

" I pray thee let me go to He-bron and pay a vow to the Lord." Da-vid let him go. Then Ab-sa-lom sent spies out to all parts of the land, to see who would take him for their king and put down Da-vid. The spies told them all that when they should hear the sound of trump-ets in the land they must shout, " Ab-sa-lom is king in He-bron."

When Da-vid was told that Is-ra-el was go-ing to join Ab-sa-lom, he was in great fear, and he fled with some of his peo-ple out of Je-ru-sa-lem. The priests brought the ark to take it with them, but Da-vid sent them back with

SHIM-E-I MOCKS AT DA-VID.

it. He said that the Lord might bring him back there,
but if not, the Lord should do to him as he saw best.
Da-vid knew how he had sinned when he had caused the
death of U-ri-ah, and so he went out of the cit-y in tears,
and all that were with him wept.

On his way a man named Shim-e-i, who was one of
Saul's kins-men, came out and mocked and cursed him.
He was glad to see Da-vid in troub-le. He threw stones
and hard words at him and his men. When Da-vid's
neph-ew want-ed to kill this man, the king would not let
him, for he said it was part of the cross that the Lord
meant him to bear for his sin. And he said, " My own
son Ab-sa-lom wants to take my life, then why may not
this man."

Now a wise man whom Da-vid had trust-ed had gone
o-ver to Ab-sa-lom. He laid plans to take Da-vid and kill
him. But there was a man named Hu-shai who sent word
to Da-vid, so that he fled and was safe.

Now when Da-vid had crossed Jor-dan, and came to
the land of Gil-e-ad, there was an old man there who
brought flour and parched corn and meat to him and his
men. In the mean time Ab-sa-lom came on with his men,
and Da-vid count-ed his troops and made Jo-ab his head·
cap-tain.

Da-vid wished to go with his men to the fight, but they
asked him not to risk his life. When they went he begged
them not to be harsh with Ab-sa-lom, for his heart was
still full of love for this bad son.

Now the fight took place in a wood, and God helped

those that fought on the side of Da-vid, and they pressed
the men of Ab-sa-lom so hard that they fled on all sides:
And a great ma-ny were slain, but more lost their lives by
fall-ing in pits and holes a-mong the rocks in the wood
than died by the sword.

Ab-sa-lom fled too, and as he fled he met some of
Da-vid's men. Now he was rid-ing on the king's mule,
and as he rode, he went un-der the boughs of a great oak
tree. As he passed be-neath the tree, his hair caught in
the boughs so that he was held be-tween the earth and
the sky, and the mule went a-way from un-der him.

One of Da-vid's men saw this, and went and told Jo-ab,
" I saw Ab-sa-lom hang in an oak tree."

Jo-ab said to the man, " Didst thou see him and not
smite him there to the ground? I would have giv-en thee
ten shek-els of sil-ver and a gir-dle."

The man said, "Though you should give me a thou-sand
shek-els of sil-ver, yet would I not put forth my hand
a-gainst the king's son; for I heard the king charge thee
and oth-ers, say-ing, Take care that no one touch the young
man Ab-sa-lom. In truth I should have wrought harm to
my-self, for there is naught hid from the king, and thou
thy-self would have set thy face a-gainst me."

Jo-ab an-swered, " I may lose no more time in talk-ing
with thee." And he took three darts in his hand, and
thrust them in-to Ab-sa-lom while he hung yet a-live in
the tree. Then ten young men, the ar-mor-bear-ers of
Jo-ab, came and made an end of him.

And Jo-ab blew a trump-et to call the peo-ple back, and

let them know that Ab-sa-lom was slain. Then the men who had been with Ab-sa-lom fled, and the oth-ers took his bod-y, and threw it in a pit, and piled stones on it.

Da-vid sat at the gate of the cit-y to hear the news. He had a watch-man on the wall to look out, and he saw a man run-ning. The man came on, and bowed down to Da-vid, and told him there was good news. The Lord had helped Da-vid's men to win. And the king asked, "Is the young man Ab-sa-lom safe?"

The man said, "I saw a great tu-mult when I left, but I knew not what it was."

Then came a sec-ond man and he said, "I have great news for my lord the king. The Lord has put thy foes to flight."

And the king asked, "Is the young man Ab-sa-lom safe?"

And the man said, "May all the king's foes, and all who wish to do him harm, be as this young man."

Then Da-vid knew his son was dead, and he was in sore grief. He went up to his room, and wept, and cried, "O Ab-sa-lom, my son, my son! Would to God that I had died for thee, O Ab-sa-lom, my son, my son!"

When Jo-ab heard how the king wept for Ab-sa-lom, he was not pleased. The peo-ple stole back to the cit-y; no one wished to see Da-vid when they knew how he grieved for his son.

But Jo-ab went to him and said, "Thou hast shamed this day the fa-ces of all thy serv-ants who have saved thy life, for in that thou lov-est thine en-e-mies more than thou lov-est them. For I see that if Ab-sa-lom had lived, and all we had died this day, then it had pleased thee well. Now there-fore rise, and go forth, and speak to thy serv-ants, or there will not one stay with thee this night, and that will be worse for thee than all the e-vil that has hap-

THE AN-GEL GOES FORTH TO SMITE THE LAND WITH PLAGUE.

pened to thee from thy youth till this time." So the king rose, and went and sat in the gate, and when the peo-ple heard of it they all came to him there.

Now the men in Je-ru-sa-lem sent word to Da-vid, "Come back to us." So he start-ed with all the men who were with him. Then Shim-e-i, who had cursed him and thrown stones, was full of fear, and he came out and fell on his face be-fore Da-vid. Then Da-vid's neph-ew said, "Shall not Shim-e-i be put to death be-cause he cursed the king?" But Da-vid said, "None should be put to death on that day, for the Lord had made him once more king of all Is-ra-el."

As he went on, old Bar-zil-la-i, who had brought him meat and flour, came out once more to meet him. The king said to him, "Come to Je-ru-sa-lem and live in my house with me, and I will take care of thee." But Bar-zil-la-i said he was an old man, and had not long to live, but if Da-vid would take his son he would be glad. The king said he would take him, and he kissed Bar-zil-la-i and blessed him.

Now the heart of Da-vid was filled with pride, and he thought his strength was in the men who fought for him, and not in the Lord. And he was moved to count his peo-ple, so that he might know how ma-ny men of war he had.

Then **Gad,** a proph-et, was sent to tell him of his sin, and to say that for his pride the Lord would send a plague on the land.

And as Da-vid was by the thrash-ing floor of A-rau-nah the Je-bu-site, he saw the an-gel of the Lord go forth to smite the land, and he and those with him fell to the ground in fear.

And Da-vid grieved, and said, "Lo, I have sinned and done wick-ed-ly; but these sheep, what have they done?

DA-VID BUILDS A NEW AL-TAR.

Let Thine hand, I pray Thee, be a-gainst me, and a-gainst my fa-ther's house."

Then Gad told Da-vid to build a new al-tar to the Lord in the thrash-ing floor of A-rau-nah, where he had seen the an-gel, that the wrath of the Lord might be ap-peased

So Da-vid bought the thrash-ing floor of A-rau-nah, and built there an al-tar, and of-fered sac-ri-fice to the Lord. And the Lord stayed the hand of the an-gel, and the plague ceased.

CHAPTER XXIII.

THE REIGN OF SOL-O-MON.

Da-vid had grown old by this time, and he knew his death was near. He had not built the house for the ark of God, for he knew his son was to do that, but he had the stones cut, and trees hewn down, and gold and sil-ver brought for the work.

And he called Sol-o-mon, his son, and told him how he had longed to build a house to the Lord, but God chose that a man of peace and not of war should build it.

Now Da-vid said he would make Sol-o-mon king while he yet lived, for he had a son named Ad-o-ni-jah who had tried to be made king. So Da-vid made Sol-o-mon ride on his own mule to a place near the cit-y, and he told the peo-ple they must blow on trump-ets and cry, "God save King Sol-o-mon," and pour the sa-cred oil on his head.

They did so, and when Ad-o-ni-jah heard the noise he asked what it was. Some one came in and said that Da-vid had made Sol-o-mon king and all were full of joy.

Then Ad-o-ni-jah was full of fear, but Sol-o-mon said that if he would do right, no harm should come to him.

Then Da-vid called the head men and prin-ces to him

and talked to them. He told them they must keep God's laws, and then they would have that good land. And he said to Sol-o-mon, "And thou, Sol-o-mon, my son, o-bey the God of thy fa-ther, and serve Him with all thy heart, for the Lord looks at the heart and knows all thy thoughts. If thou serve Him, He will be thy friend; but if thou turn from Him, He will cast thee off."

He gave Sol-o-mon all he had for the house of the ark, and told him the Lord would help him build it. And he called the peo-ple and asked them to give al-so. So they brought gold, and sil-ver, and brass, and rich gems, and gave them to the Lord.

Then Da-vid prayed for them, that they might love Sol-o-mon and keep his laws. They made a feast, and ate and drank to the Lord, and of-fered up ma-ny beasts to Him. So Sol-o-mon ruled the land, and Da-vid died and they bur-ied him at Je-ru-sa-lem.

Now Sol-o-mon feared God. The Lord spoke to him in a dream at night and said, "Ask what I shall give thee." Sol-o-mon asked that he might be made wise so that he would rule the peo-ple well.

God was pleased that Sol-o-mon had not asked for wealth or long life, and He said He would make him wise and give him all the rest of the good gifts too.

Now Sol-o-mon had to judge the peo-ple, and there came to him two wo-men who had lived in one house. One of them said, "O, my lord, this wo-man and I live in one house, and we each had a son. Her child died in the night, and she rose up while I slept, and took my son from me, and laid it in her bed, and put her dead child in my bed. And when I woke to feed my child, it was dead, and I looked and it was not my child."

The oth-er wo-man said, "Nay the liv-ing child is mine!"

So the king said, " Bring a sword." They brought it. And the king said, "Cut the liv-ing child in two, and give half to each." Then the real moth-er, who loved the child too well to see it killed, cried out, " O, my lord, give her the child—do not kill it." The oth-er did not care, and said, "Cut it in two." Then the king knew which was the true moth-er, and he said that the one who had begged for its life should keep it.

So the peo-ple knew that he was a wise king. God made him rich and great. Sol-o-mon sent word to Hi-ram, king of Tyre, who had been a friend of Da-vid's, that he want-ed his men to hew down ce-dar trees on Leb-a-non. They brought them to the sea, and made them in rafts, and float-ed them down to Je-ru-sa-lem.

So they laid out the plan of a great house. It was to be built of stone. Each stone was cut and made for its own place. When the walls were built they had ce-dar carved with flow-ers laid on them. The in-side of the porch was lined with pure gold, and a rich blue and pur-ple and crim-son cur-tain hung in the house to make two rooms of it. This was called the veil. The in-most place was called " Most Ho-ly," and it was in-laid with gold, with two cher-u-bim cov-ered with gold. These cher-u-bim had their wings spread out, and their fa-ces turned to the wall. The doors were made of fir trees and carved

SOL-O-MON'S WISE JUDG-MENT.

and gild-ed. And there was a great brass ba-sin, and a
brass al-tar four times as large as the one Mo-ses had
made. And he set ten can-dle-sticks of gold on the al-tar
to light the place. He spent sev-en years build-ing this
house.

Then Sol-o-mon sent for all the chief men of Is-ra-el to
come and see the ark brought to the house. The priests
took the ark and set it in the most ho-ly place, and·the
glo-ry of the Lord filled the house like a cloud.

Then Sol-o-mon thanked them all for that they had

helped him build the house, and he prayed God to take
that house for His Tem-ple.   He knelt down, and asked
God to hear all the pray-ers that the chil-dren of Is-ra-el
should make in that house.

When he had spo-ken, fire came down from heav-en
and burnt the of-fer-ing that lay on the al-tar.   Then all the
peo-ple fell on their fa-ces and prayed.   And a great feast
was held there for two weeks.

The Lord spoke to Sol-o-mon in the night, and said He
would take the house to be His Tem-ple.   He said if the
peo-ple sinned and would come there and pray He would
for-give them.   If Sol-o-mon kept His law, he should be
king as long as he lived, and his sons aft-er him ; but if
he served oth-er gods, he would be driv-en out, and his
foes would lay waste the Tem-ple.

Sol-o-mon built a grand pal-ace in Je-ru-sa-lem, and
cit-ies to hold his great wealth.

The queen of a far off land called She-ba heard how
wise and great he was, and she came to see him.   She
brought spice, and gold, and gems, as gifts.   She saw the
great Tem-ple, and the wealth on all sides, and she said
the half had not been told her.   She asked Sol-o-mon hard
ques-tions, and he made all plain to her.   She went back
to her own land load-ed with rich gifts.

The throne of Sol-o-mon was made of i-vo-ry covered
with pure gold, and he had six li-ons made to stand on
each side, and all his cups and dish-es were made of gold.
He sent ships out that brought him back all sorts of rich
things.

THE QUEEN OF SHE-BA COMES TO SEE SOL-O-MON.

But Sol-o-mon sinned in that he took wives who served strange gods. They led him to for-get God. Then the Lord raised up foes to troub-le him.

There was a young man of Is-ra-el named Jer-o-bo-am. He met a proph-et one day who told him the Lord meant to make him king of Is-ra-el. When Sol-o-mon heard this he tried to kill Jer-o-bo-am, but he fled to E-gypt.

When Sol-o-mon died the peo-ple sent word to Jer-o-bo-am, and he came back. Now Sol-o-mon had a son named Re-ho-bo-am. The peo-ple came to him and said that if he would say he would be kind to them, and not be cru-el as his fa-ther he should rule them, and they would serve him.

Re-ho-bo-am asked the old men what he should do, and they told him that he should tell the peo-ple he would be kind. But the young men told him to be stern and hard.

So Re-ho-bo-am took his young friends' ad-vice. When the men came to him he was rough with them, and said he would be more cru-el than his fa-ther.

So Is-ra-el was an-gry, and said he should not be king, and they chose Jer-o-bo-am. But the tribes of Ju-dah and Ben-ja-min kept Re-ho-bo-am for their king.

When he saw what his harsh words had done he wished to call the peo-ple back, but they stoned the men he sent to them. Then he called his men to go out and fight, but the Lord sent them word they must not go, so they went back to their own homes. So now there were two kings who ruled Is-ra-el.

CHAPTER XXIV.

THE WID-OW'S OIL AND MEAL.

Now . Jer-o-bo-am feared that when the chil-dren of Is-ra-el went up to Je-ru-sa-lem to pray, and saw there the son of Sol-o-mon as king, they might not keep their vow to him. · So he had two calves of gold made, and set them up in the land, and said to the peo-ple that it was too far to go to Je-ru-sa-lem and they could pray to these calves. He built a house for the calves, and made feasts for them, and chose bad men to be priests for these i-dols.

Then the priests and Le-vites left the land, and all who would not bow down to the calves; and they went to Je-ru-sa-lem and served Re-ho-bo-am as their king.

One day, as Jer-o-bo-am stood by one of these i-dols to burn in-cense, a man of God from Ju-dah came to him, and told him that a king should be born in Ju-dah that would spoil that al-tar; and as a sign that his word was true, on that. ver-y day the al-tar should be brok-en.

Jer-o-bo-am, in great wrath, strove to seize the man of God, but his arm grew stiff so that he could not move it. The al-tar was brok-en and the ash-es spilled.

Then Jer-o-bo-am begged the man of God to pray that his hand might be made well, and he did so. Then the king begged him to go home with him, but he would not. He said the Lord had told him not to eat bread or drink wa-ter till he was home once more.

Now there was an old man in Beth-el who was a proph-et too, and he made haste and went out and met the man of God from Ju-dah. He told him that God had sent him, and said, " Bring him back with thee that he may eat and drink."

Now this was false, and the proph-et from Ju-dah should not have gone with him. But he did so, and ate and drank, and the Lord was an-gry with him. The word of

God came to the old proph-et, and he told the man from Ju-dah that he should not reach his home, and that his grave should be in a strange land.

And so it came to pass. As he start-ed for home a li-on met him and slew him. Some men who saw it told the old proph-et who lived in Beth-el, and he took an ass and rode out to the place. There lay the dead bod-y and the li-on stood by it. The proph-et took up the bod-y and buried it in his own place. And he said to his sons, "When I die, lay me by the bod-y of the proph-et from Ju-dah."

Now a son of Jer-o-bo-am grew sick, and Jer-o-bo-am asked his wife to dress so that no one should know she was queen, and go to the proph-et in Shi-loh who had told him he should be made king. She must take gifts and find out if the child would get well.

The wife of Jer-o-bo-am did so. The proph-et was old, and his sight was dim, but the Lord told him who had come. So when he heard her he said, "Come in thou wife of Jer-o-bo-am, it is in vain to try to hide thy-self from me, for the Lord hath said, 'Go say to Jer-o-bo-am, I raised thee up and made thee king, but thou hast done e-vil and made oth-er gods. So I will send e-vil on thee and thine till not one is left, and when they are dead they shall not lie in graves.' Go back to thine own house, but as thou go-est, the child shall die. The peo-ple shall mourn for him, for he is the last of Jer-o-bo-am's house that shall lie in a grave." And it came to pass as the man of God said; for as the wife of Jer-o-bo-am went in the door of her own house, the child died.

Then Jer-o-bo-am died, and his son reigned in his stead. He did wrong in God's sight, and there were five more bad kings. They served false gods, and bowed down to calves of gold. We are told that A-hab was the worst of all these kings. His wife was the child of a hea-then king, and served a god named Ba-al. A-hab built a house for this i-dol, and had men that he called priests of Ba-al, and he made Is-ra-el bow down to Ba-al. Then the Lord was wroth with A-hab, and sent the proph-et E-li-jah to tell him that he should not be king, and that no rain should fall in the land for years. This would make a fam-ine in the land, so the Lord told E-li-jah where he could go and hide by a brook that was out in a wild place. The Lord sent ra-vens with meat and bread to him each day, and he

E-LI-JAH FED BY RA-VENS.

drank from the brook. But at last the brook dried up toc for want of rain.

Then the Lord told him to go to a city named Zar-e-phath, where there was a wo-man who would feed him. E-li-jah went, and saw a wo-man pick-ing up sticks. He said to her, " Bring me, I pray thee, a lit-tle wa-ter in a cup, that I may drink." As she turned to go he said, " Bring me, I pray thee, a piece of bread."

Then the wo-man said, " As the Lord liv-eth, I have no bread, but on-ly a hand-ful of meal and a lit-tle oil, and I am get-ting a few sticks that I may bake it for me and my son, that we may not die."

Then E-li-jah said, " Fear not; bake it as thou hast said, but make me a lit-tle cake first." Then he told her the Lord had said the meal and oil should last as long as the fam-ine last-ed in the land.

So the wo-man had faith, and did as he said. She took the proph-et home, and they all lived on the oil and meal for a year, for the Lord made it last.

The son of the wo-man grew sick and died. She came to E-li-jah and told of her great grief. He said, " Give me thy son." And he took him and laid him on his own bed, and cried to the Lord to save him and bring back his life to him. And the Lord was pleased to do as E-li-jah asked him, and the soul of the child came back to him, and he lived. E-li-jah took him and laid him in his moth-er's arms.

CHAPTER XXV.

Now Jez-e-bel, the wife of A-hab, hat-ed all the men of God in the land, and want-ed to have them killed. Then the chief of A-hab's house, a good man named O-ba-di-ah, hid them in caves, and sent them food and drink.

Now the fam-ine had last-ed three years, when A-hab called O-ba-di-ah, and sent him out to see if he could find some springs hid in the grass, so that the cat-tle might not die. O-ba-di-ah went, and on his way E-li-jah came to meet him. O-ba-di-ah fell on his face, and E-li-jah told him to go and tell A-hab he was there. But O-ba-di-ah feared to do this. He told E-li-jah how A-hab had sought for him, and now he said, "The Lord will car-ry thee a-way, and when A-hab shall come and not find thee, he will kill me."

But E-li-jah said, "As the Lord liv-eth I will show my-self to A-hab this day."

So O-ba-di-ah went, and A-hab came forth to meet E-li-jah. He blamed him for the want in the land. But E-li-jah told him it was caused by him and his peo-ple, who had turned from God and served Ba-al.

Then E-li-jah told him to bring all the peo-ple to Mount Car-mel, and they should see who was the true God. He told them to lay an of-fer-ing on Ba-al's al-tar and put no fire un-der it, and he would lay one on God's al-tar and

put no fire un-der it, and they would see which would be
burned. They did so, and the priests of Ba-al called on
him, but no fire came. Then E-li-jah had wa-ter poured
o-ver the wood on the al-tar of the Lord, and he prayed,
and fire came down from the Lord and burnt the wood.

When the peo-ple saw it, they cried out, "The Lord
He is God, the Lord He is God."

And E-li-jah said, "Take the priests of Ba-al—let not
one of them live." For the Lord had said it.

Then E-li-jah went to the top of Mount Car-mel, and
prayed to God to send rain. He sent his man to look to
the sea, but at first he saw no sign. At last he came back
and said, " I see a small cloud as large as a man's hand."

Then E-li-jah sent word to A-hab to ride home as fast
as he could or the storm would come on him. The cloud
grew, and the sky was black, and there was a great rain.

When Jez-e-bel heard of all this, she was in a great
rage. She sent word to E-li-jah, " Let the gods slay me
too, if I do not put thee to death."

When E-li-jah heard this he fled. He was so tired and
weak with his flight that he asked the Lord to let him die.
As he slept, an an-gel touched him, and showed him a
cake and a cruse of wa-ter. And the Lord gave him food
twice, so that he might be strong.

And he went a long way and hid in a cave. Then a
great storm came there, and a wind that tore up the earth,
and a great earth-quake that shook the ground, and a fire,
but the Lord was not in all these. Then there came a still
small voice. And E-li-jah knew that God spoke to him.

And the Lord asked, "What do-est thou here, E-li-jah?" Then E-li-jah told Him.

But the Lord said, "I have yet sev-en thou-sand per-sons in the land of Is-ra-el who have not bowed the knee to Ba-al." And He told him to go back, and to a-noint E-li-sha to take his place as proph-et, for the time would soon come when his work would be done.

So E-li-jah went, and he saw E-li-sha in a field at the plough. As he passed he threw his man-tle on E-li-sha, and the Lord showed E-li-sha what he meant. So he left the plough, and ran aft-er E-li-jah, and said, "Let me go and take leave of my fa-ther and moth-er and I will come to thee." He did so, and then went with E-li-jah to serve him.

Now the king of a coun-try called Syr-i-a made war on A-hab, and he sent word to the chief men of Is-ra-el. The Lord helped him, though the force of the Syr-i-ans' was large.

The Syr-i-ans tried more, and though the Is-ra-el-ites were but a hand-ful, the Lord made them win the fight. The king of Syr-i-a fled and hid in a house. His serv-ants went to A-hab to beg him to spare their king's life.

So the king was brought out, and A-hab took him up in his own char-i-ot, and spared his life. For the king of Syr-i-a had told him he would give him some of his cit-ies. The Lord was not pleased that A-hab had done this, and He sent word to him, "Thy life shall go for his life, and thou shalt be slain in-stead of him."

Now there was a man named Na-both who had a vine-

yard near the pal-ace of the king. A-hab wished him to
sell it that he might have a gar-den there, and he told him
he would give him land or mon-ey for it. But Na-both
would not sell it for it was his home and had been his
fa-ther's. A-hab was an-gry at this, for he had set his
heart on the land. He would not eat, and Je-ze-bel came
and asked him, "Why art thou so sad?" He told her,
and she said, "Art thou king to be treat-ed so? Rise up
eat, drink, and be mer-ry; I will give thee the vine-yard."

She made a plot to have Na-both killed. She got some
bad men to tell lies and say he had said wrong things of
God and the king. So Na-both was stoned to death and
A-hab took his vine-yard.

When E-li-jah heard this he went out to meet A-hab.
Then A-hab cried out, "Hast thou found me, O my
en-e-my?"

E-li-jah said, "I have found thee, for thou hast sinned
a-gainst the Lord."

Then the man of God told A-hab that he and all in his
house should be killed, and the dogs would eat Jez-e-bel
his wife, for she had caused him to sin.

So A-hab went up with the chil-dren of Is-ra-el to take
one of the cit-ies which the king of Syr-i-a had said he
would give him. There was a fight, and A-hab was
struck with a dart in the breast. He died, and the men
of Is-ra-el fled.

His son A-ha-zi-ah came to the throne, and he did e-vil
in the sight of the Lord. It came to pass that he fell and
was hurt, and he sent to ask of his i-dol if he would get

well. Then the Lord said to E-li-jah, "Go up and meet the men, and say to them, "Is there no God in Is-ra-el that ye go and ask the i-dol of the Phil-is-tines? Now, there-fore, the Lord hath said that the king shall not rise up from that bed, and he shall sure-ly die."

They went back and told this to the king, and he was an-gry. He sent out fif-ty men to take E-li-jah, but the man of God prayed, and said, "If I be a proph-et, let fire come down and burn up these men." And it came to pass that the chief man and all who were with him were burnt with fire. When the king heard this he sent more men, but they met the same fate. Then the third time the king sent men, but when they came to the place, the chief fell on his knees and begged E-li-jah to spare them.

So the an-gel of the Lord said to E-li-jah, "Go with him : do not fear."

Then E-li-jah went with him to the king, and told him, "Thus saith the Lord. Be-cause thou sent to ask of the i-dol of the Phil-is-tines, thou shalt not rise up from that bed, and thou shalt die."

CHAPTER XXVI.

THE STO-RY OF E-LI-SHA.

Now when the time came for the Lord to take E-li-jah, he went with E-li-sha to a place called Gil-gal. He said to E-li-sha, "Stay here, for the Lord hath sent me to Beth-el."

But E-li-sha would not leave him, and they went on

to Beth-el. The young men came to E-li-sha and said, " Know-est thou that the Lord will take thy mas-ter from thee to day?"

And he said, "Yes I know it, hold ye your peace."

Then E-li-jah said, "Stay at Beth-el, I pray thee, for the Lord hath sent me to Jer-i-cho." But E-li-sha would not leave him. He went with him to Jer-i-cho, and then on to Jor-dan. The young men from the schools went aft-er them, as they stood by the side of the riv-er. And E-li-jah took off his man-tle and struck the wa-ter, and it part-ed and made a dry path for them to cross.

Then E-li-jah said to E-li-sha, "Ask what I shall do for thee, be-fore I be tak-en from thee."

Then E-li-sha asked that he might have more of God's spir-it in his heart.

Then E-li-jah said, "Thou hast asked a hard thing. Yet if thou see me when I am tak-en from thee, thou shalt have thy wish."

So they walked on. Then all at once a char-i-ot of fire, and hor-ses of fire, came and took E-li-jah from the sight of his friend.

And E-li-sha cried out, "My fa-ther, my fa-ther, the char-i-ot of Is-ra-el, and the horse-men there-of!" Then he rent his clothes, and he took the man-tle that E-li-jah had left, and struck the wa-ters of the Jor-dan, and they part-ed and he went o-ver on dry land.

Then the young men came, and bowed down to him, and said, " Let us go, we pray thee, and look for thy mas-ter. It may be the Lord has left him on some mount

E-LI-JAH IS TAK-EN UP IN A CHAR-I-OT.

or in some val-ley." At first E-li-sha said, "no;" but when they begged him, he said, "go."

But they could not find E-li-jah.

The men of Jer-i-cho came to E-li-sha and said that the wa-ter in their land was bad, and crops would not grow there. So E-li-sha sent for a new cruse, and put salt in it, and threw it in the spring, and said, "Thus saith the Lord, I have made the wa-ter pure." And so it was from that day.

Now as E-li-sha went to Beth-el, some lit-tle ones came forth, and mocked him, and said, "Go up, thou bald head." E-li-sha turned and looked at them, and he prayed God to pun-ish them for their sin. Then two bears came out and tore for-ty-two of them.

Now Is-ra-el went out to fight the men of Mo-ab, and they marched sev-en days, and found no wa-ter. Then one asked, "Is there no proph-et here who can pray to the Lord for us?" And it was said, "E-li-sha is here."

So they went to E-li-sha, and he told them to dig ditch-es in the camp, and they would be filled with wa-ter. Then they must take the cit-ies of Mo-ab, and cut down the trees, and spoil the land. And it came to pass, as he said, that the ditch-es were full of wa-ter the next day.

Now the men of Mo-ab brought all their for-ces to the camp of Is-ra-el. And it came to pass that the sun shone on the ditch-es, and made the wa-ter look as red as blood. Then the men of Mo-ab thought that Is-ra-el had fought with one an-oth-er, and all they had to do was to go and take the spoil. But when they saw the ar-my they fled, and Is-ra-el went aft-er them, and took them and their cit-ies, and spoiled the land.

Then a wo-man cried to E-li-sha that her hus-band had died while he owed mon-ey he could not pay. The man to whom he owed it had come to take her two sons to serve for the mon-ey like slaves. E-li-sha said, "What hast thou in thy house?" She said, "I have noth-ing but a pot of oil."

Then he told her to ask all her friends to lend her pots

and dish-es, and to pour them full of oil, and set them on one side. She did so, and her sons went far and wide, and brought dish-es to her to fill.

She poured and poured, but the oil still came. She said to her sons, "Bring more," but they said, "There is not one more."

Then E-li-sha said, "Go sell the oil, and pay the man what thou ow-est him, and then buy food for thee and thy chil-dren."

Now there was a rich and good wo-man in the town of Shu-nem who loved to have E-li-sha come to her house. She built him a room, and set in it a bed, a ta-ble, a stool, and a can-dle-stick, so that he could make his home there when he chose.

Once when he was there, he told her she had been so kind to him that he would like to know if there was a-ny-thing he could ask for her from the king. But she said she need-ed noth-ing. Then Ge-ha-zi, his serv-ant, said, "She has no child." E-li-sha said, "Call her." And she came. Then the proph-et told her the Lord would give her a son. And in time a boy was born to her. When he was large he went out one day to the field to the reap-ers. And he grew sick and cried out, "My head, my head." His fa-ther told one of the young men to take him to his moth-er, and he did so. The boy sat in her lap till noon, and then he died. She took him to E-li-sha's room, and laid him on his bed. Then she made haste and rode to find the proph-et at Mount Car-mel. He saw her a long way off, and sent Ge-ha-zi to meet her, and ask her, "Is it

well with thee? Is it well with thy hus-band? Is it well
with the child?" She said, "It is well."

Then she drew near, and fell on the ground, and clasped
the feet of E-li-sha, and cried, "Did I ask that I might
have a son?" Then E-li-sha knew that the boy was dead.
And he gave his staff to Ge-ha-zi, and told him to make
great haste, and speak to no one, but to go and lay the
staff on the face of the child.

But the wo-man would not go with-out E-li-sha. So he
rose up and went with her. He met Ge-ha-zi, who said,
"The child has not waked."

Then E-li-sha went to his room where the child lay
dead on the bed. He shut the door and prayed. Then
he got up and put his mouth on the child's mouth, and his
eyes on the child's eyes, and his hands on the child's hands,
and the boy's flesh grew warm. He went out and walked
for a while, and then he did the same thing once more,
and the child came to life. Then he called the moth-er
and laid the boy in her arms.

E-li-sha did ma-ny things with the Lord's help. He
changed a poi-son vine to good food, and he made a few
loaves feed a hun-dred men so that there was some left.

Now there was a brave man in Syr-i-a called Na-a-man,
and he was a lep-er. A lit-tle maid from Is-ra-el who
served Na-a-man's wife told her of a proph-et in her own
land who could cure him.

Then the king of Syr-i-a sent Na-a-man to the king of
Is-ra-el with a let-ter. And he took gold pie-ces to pay
for his cure. But the king of Is-ra-el said, "Am I God,

that I can cure a lep-er?" He thought the king of Syr-i-a want-ed an ex-cuse to make war on him, and he rent his clothes, and was troub-led.

When E-li-sha heard this, he sent word to him, " Let the man come to me and he shall know there is a proph-et in Is-ra-el."

So Na-a-man, with his grand char-i-ot and hor-ses, came to E-li-sha's door. The proph-et sent word to him, " Go wash sev-en times in the riv-er Jor-dan and thou shalt be clean."

Now Na-a-man was in a rage. He thought that the riv-ers in his own land were as good as a-ny in Is-ra-el. Then the man of God had not e-ven come out to look at him. But his serv-ants were more wise than he. They came to him and said, " If the proph-et had asked thee to do some hard thing, thou wouldst have done it. But now when he says, ' Wash and be clean,' thou wilt not."

So Na-a-man went and dipped sev-en times in the riv-er Jor-dan, and his flesh grew soft and pure as a lit-tle child's.

Then he went back in great joy to the house of E-li-sha, and wished to give him rich gifts, but the proph-et would take none.

Then Na-a-man asked for as much earth as two mules could bear. He wished to take it to his own land that he might build an al-tar to the true God, and pray to Him from that day. But Na-a-man told E-li-sha that when his mas-ter the king went to the i-dol's house to pray, he would have to go with him and let him lean on his arm.

He asked if the Lord would for-give him for that. He

might seem to bow down to the i-dol, but he would pray
to the Lord in his heart. And E-li-sha said, "Go in peace."

So Na-a-man went on his way. Now Ge-ha-zi thought,
"Why should I not take a gift from this man?" So he
ran aft-er him, and said, "My mas-ter sent me to tell thee
that there are two young men come to him who are sons
of the proph-ets. He asks thee to give them a piece of
sil-ver and two chan-ges of clothes." Then Na-a-man took
two pie-ces of sil-ver, and two suits of clothes, and put
them in two bags, and gave them to two of his men to
car-ry. When they came to E-li-sha's house Ge-ha-zi took
them and hid them. Then he went in to his mas-ter.

Now E-li-sha knew all the man had done, for the Lord
had told him. So he asked him, "Where hast thou been,
Ge-ha-zi?" The man said, "Thy serv-ant hath been no
where." Then E-li-sha said, "Did I not know it when
Na-a-man came down from his char-i-ot to meet thee? Is
this a time to take mon-ey, and gar-ments, and rich-es?
There-fore, be-cause thou hast done this thing, the lep-ro-sy
which Na-a-man has been cured of shall be on thee, and
on thy chil-dren for-ev-er!"

And it was so, for Ge-ha-zi went out a lep-er as white
as snow.

Then the sons of the proph-ets came to E-li-sha and
said the house where they lived was too small for them.
So they begged E-li-sha to go with them to the riv-er Jor-
dan, while they cut down trees there that they might build
a lar-ger house. And the top of the axe that one of them
used fell in the wa-ter. He was in great grief, for it was

not his own, but E-li-sha made the i-ron float on the wa-ter so that he could pick it up.

Now the Lord made known to E-li-sha that Ben-ha-dad, the king of Syr-i-a, meant to make war on Is-ra-el, and take their king. E-li-sha told the king of Is-ra-el, and he fled. When Ben-ha-dad could not find him, he thought

E-LI-SHA MAKES THE AXE FLOAT.

some man in his own camp must have warned him. He called his men and asked which one was a friend to the king of Is-ra-el. One said, "None of us is on his side, O king. It is E-li-sha, the proph-et, who tells him the words thou dost speak."

Then the king of Syr-i-a said, "Go and find out where
E-li-sha is, that I may take him." So they found that he
was in the cit-y of Do-than. Then Ben-ha-dad sent men
and hor-ses to Do-than. E-li-sha's serv-ant saw them, and
he was in great fright, but his mas-ter said, "Fear not,
they that are with us are more than they that are a-gainst
us." He prayed to the Lord, and all at once a great host
seemed to camp round the place as a guard to E-li-sha.
Then, when Ben-ha-dad's men came to take him, E-li-sha
prayed that they might be made blind.

The Lord heard E-li-sha, and it was so that the men
could not see. Then E-li-sha led them straight to the king
of Is-ra-el, and prayed to the Lord to make them see, and
He did so, and they saw where they were.

The king asked E-li-sha what he should do to the men,
and he told him to give them food and send them back to
their own land.

Then Ben-ha-dad laid siege to the cit-y of Sa-ma-ri-a,
and would let no bread go in, so that the peo-ple were
starved.

When the king saw this, he blamed E-li-sha, and wished
to kill him, but E-li-sha told him that the next day there
would be food for all.

That same night the Lord caused the Syr-i-ans to think
that a great host was com-ing to fight them. So they left
their tents, and all that they had, and fled. Then the
Is-ra-el-ites came up, and the food, and gold, and rich
clothes that the Syr-i-ans had left all fell in-to their hands.

CHAPTER XXVII.

In due time the Lord brought to pass the doom which He had said by the mouth of E-li-jah should fall on the chil-dren of A-hab.

He caused E-li-sha to have a young man named Je-hu a-noint-ed as king of Is-ra-el. Je-hu was told that he must kill all who were left of the house of A-hab, who had done e-vil in the sight of the Lord.

Je-hu went at once to Jez-reel with his men. He met King Je-ho-ram at the gate, and drew his bow and shot him so that he fell dead. They left his bod-y on the ground, in the place that had once been Na-both's vine-yard.

Now Jez-e-bel had paint-ed her face, and put on fine clothes, and she sat in a win-dow as Je-hu and his men marched in. He looked up, and said to some of the men of the house, " Who is on my side, throw her down to me." They threw her down and the hor-ses trod her un-der foot.

When Je-hu sent his men to bring her, they could on-ly find her skull and some bones, for the dogs had eat-en her, as the Lord had said. So there was no one left of the house of A-hab.

Je-hu did e-vil in God's sight, and he left a son who was just as bad. So the Lord let Haz-a-el, who had slain Ben-ha-dad and made him-self king of Syr-i-a, fight

DEATH OF JEZ-E-BEL.

Is-ra-el, and burn their cit-ies, and kill the young men and maid-ens and lit-tle chil-dren.

Now E-li-sha had grown sick, and was near his death. Je-ho-ash, who was then king of Is-ra-el, came to him, and stood by his bed, and wept. Then E-li-sha told the king to take a bow, and shoot an ar-row to the east. He did so, and E-li-sha told him that he should set Is-ra-el free from the Syr-i-ans.

Then E-li-sha told the king to take the ar-rows in his hand, and strike on the ground with them.

The king struck three times, and then stopped. E-li-sha

told him that if he had not stopped he would have led Is-ra-el in a war that would have put an end to the Syr-i-ans, but now he would win on-ly three fights.

Then E-li-sha died and was bur-ied. Now it came to pass that some Mo-ab-ites who came to rob, met men who bore a corpse to its grave. The men were in such fear that they did not take the dead man to the grave that had been dug for him, but put him in the one where E-li-sha had been placed. As soon as the corpse touched the bones of E-li-sha, life came back to it, and the man rose and stood on his feet.

King Je-ho-ash won three fights with the Syr-i-ans, as E-li-sha had said, and then he died and his son Jer-o-bo-am reigned in his stead. The Lord still helped Is-ra-el, but they would not serve him, but bowed down to calves of gold. A-mos, the proph-et, went to talk to them, and tell them what the Lord had done for them, and how they had sinned.

But King Jer-o-bo-am would not hear the words of the proph-et, and went on with his sins, and so did his sons, and his sons' sons. They would not serve God, but set up false gods in high pla-ces and made their sons and daugh-ters go through the fire to please these i-dols.

So at last God drove the Is-ra-el-ites out of Ca-naan, as he had done with the na-tions that lived there be-fore them. The king of As-syr-i-a went through the land and drove them out, and took all the ten tribes with him to his land, and they had to serve him.

CHAPTER XXVIII.

Now Sol-o-mon's son Re-ho-bo-am, we know, had been made king at Je-ru-sa-lem o-ver the tribes of Ju-dah and Ben-ja-min. The priests and Le-vites who would not bow down to the gold-en calves came there, and made the king-dom strong. For a time Re-ho-bo-am served the Lord, and all went well, but then he and the rest of the peo-ple made i-dols, and set them in high pla-ces. Then the Lord sent the king of E-gypt to fight them. ·

A proph-et came and told the king of Ju-dah that the Lord would not help him be-cause he had sinned. He bowed his head and owned that he had done wrong. Then the Lord did not let the E-gyp-tians kill him, but they took what they chose of gold and sil-ver out of the land.

When A-sa was king of Ju-dah he did what was right, and pleased God. Yet in his old age he tried to buy peace from his foe with sil-ver and gold, and did not trust in the Lord. He died, and his son Je-hosh-a-phat reigned in his stead.

He did what was right in the sight of God and he was blessed and made rich. He sent men out through all the towns of Ju-dah with the book of God's laws, so that they might teach them to all.

When the na-tions came to fight him, he called the peo-ple to fast and pray. And he asked help of the Lord,

who sent word to him not to fear. And the Lord made
the na-tions that had come to make war fight one with
an-oth-er. When the men of Ju-dah came near, they saw
all their foes dead on the ground, and they had more gold
and sil-ver than they could take a-way.

Je-hosh-a-phat had sev-en sons, and to six he left gold
and sil-ver, and cit-ies for them to rule, but his first born
son, Je-ho-ram, was made king. He turned to i-dols and
sinned in God's sight. Then he killed all his broth-ers
for fear they would take the land from him.

The Lord sent a sore sick-ness on him so that he died.

His son A-ha-zi-ah reigned for one year. His moth-er
was the daugh-ter of A-hab and she led him to do that
which was not right.

He was shot by Je-hu, and when his moth-er knew he
was dead she took his sons and slew them so that she
might be queen.

But there was one lit-tle boy named Jo-ash that the
good high priest hid in the tem-ple. When he had been
hid-den for six years, the high priest brought him out and
the Le-vites made him king.

Then they seized the wick-ed queen, and took her to a
place near and slew her.

While Je-hoi-a-da, the high priest who had hid-den him
so long, lived, Jo-ash did that which was right. But he
had no true love for God in his heart, and when Je-hoi-a-da
died he gave the prin-ces of Ju-dah leave to stay a-way
from the tem-ple, and they turned back to their i-dols.

Then the Lord sent the Syr-i-ans to make war, and they

won the fight.   Jo-ash fell sick and his own serv-ants killed him in his bed.

His son Am-a-zi-ah reigned in his stead.   He made war on the E-dom-ites, and the Lord helped him to win the fight.   But when he came home, he brought the i-dols of the E-dom-ites with him, and set them up to be his gods, and bowed down to them.

A proph-et came to him and asked him, "Why dost thou pray to the i-dols of E-dom that could not help them when thou didst fight them?"

Then Am-a-zi-ah was an-gry, and said, "Art thou here to tell me what I must do?" and he said he would put the proph-et in pris-on if he would not keep still.

Then the proph-et told him that God would make an end of him, and it came to pass.   He went out to fight a-gainst Is-ra-el, and the king of Is-ra-el took him cap-tive back to Je-ru-sa-lem, and broke down the wall of the cit-y, and went in the tem-ple and took the gold and sil-ver that were there.   Then Am-a-zi-ah was killed by some of his own peo-ple who did not want him for their king.

Uz-zi-ah, his son, came next to the throne.   At first he did what was right.   But he grew proud of his strength, and thought he could do as he chose.   He went in a part of the tem-ple where none but priests should go, and for this was made a lep-er, and stayed a lep-er till he died.

When he died, his son Jo-tham was king, and he served God.   But the peo-ple served i-dols, and God sent I-sa-iah to talk to them.   He warned them, but they would not hear.   He told them that their foes should make slaves of

them, and he spoke of Christ who would be born of the
tribe of Ju-dah to save the world from sin.

Then the good king died, and his son A-haz reigned.
He was a bad man and served strange gods. He had the
doors of the tem-ple shut so that no one could go there to
pray, and he set up i-dols in all the cit-ies of the land.

When he died he was not laid in the grave of kings, for
the Lord was ver-y an-gry at the e-vil he had done.

Hez-e-ki-ah, his son, was made king, and he made haste
to have the tem-ple o-pened and cleaned, and the al-tars set
up, and he went with the priests to of-fer up a burnt of-fer-
ing and sing prais-es to God with harps and cym-bals.

And he wrote let-ters and sent men with them to all
parts of the land for peo-ple to come and keep the feast to
the Lord. Most of the men of Is-ra-el mocked at them,
but the men of Ju-dah went up to keep the feast of the
Pass-o-ver.

When they had kept the feast, they went out through
the land and broke in pie-ces all the i-dols they found
there. So King Hez-e-ki-ah kept all the laws of God.

When the King of As-syr-i-a came and took some of the
cit-ies of the land, Hez-e-ki-ah made the walls of Je-ru-sa-
lem strong. He met his peo-ple and said, "Do not fear,
for God will fight for us."

The King of As-syr-i-a sent word to the peo-ple of Je-ru-
sa-lem not to trust the word of their king, but to make
friends with him and he would do no harm to them.
When Hez-e-ki-ah heard this, he rent his clothes and went
up to the tem-ple to pray to the Lord. And that night

the Lord sent an an-gel in-to the camp of the As-syr-i-ans and slew them.

Hez-e-ki-ah was one of the best kings of Ju-dah. He fell sick once, and the proph-et I-sa-iah told him that it was the Lord's will that he should die. But Hez-e-ki-ah prayed to the Lord, and the Lord heard him, and sent I-sa-iah to say to him that He would add fif-teen years to his life.

When Hez-e-ki-ah died, his son Ma-nas-seh was made king. He did e-vil, and prayed to be sun, moon, and stars.

He caused the peo-ple to sin. The Lord spoke to him by His proph-ets, but he would not hear. He was bound and led in chains to Bab-y-lon.

Then he thought of the Lord and prayed to him with all his heart, and the Lord helped him, and let him go back to Je-ru-sa-lem, and from that time he served the true God. But when he died, his son Am-mon did wrong in the sight of God, and he was killed by his own serv-ants.

CHAPTER XXIX.

JE-RU-SA-LEM IS LAID WASTE.

Jo-si-ah was but a boy when he was made king, but he served the Lord. He threw down the al-tars of Ba-al, and built up the tem-ple, and the Lord said that He would not pun-ish the Is-ra-el-ites for their sins in his day.

Jo-si-ah went through the land and threw down the gold-en calves, and made a feast to the Lord. He asked all his peo-ple to come to this feast, and they came, but they did not love the Lord in their hearts. When Jer-e-mi-ah talked to them of their sins, they said, " Let us kill him," but the Lord saved him.

The king of E-gypt made war on the Is-ra-el-ites, and Jo-si-ah was killed. His son was made king, but he did e-vil in the Lord's sight, and the E-gyp-tians bound him in chains and took him to E-gypt. He died there. Je-hoi-a-kim was made king, but he had to do just as the king of E-gypt told him.

Then the Lord told Jer-e-mi-ah to write down in a book all the woes He meant to bring on Is-ra-el for their sins. So Ba-ruch, who was a scribe or wri-ter, did this, and he took the book to the tem-ple to read it where all the peo-ple could hear. Those who heard it told the king of the book, and he sent for it so that he might hear. He was an-gry when he heard it, and cut out all the leaves of the book, and burnt them in the fire. He tried to find Jer-e-mi-ah and Ba-ruch to kill them, but the Lord saved them.

Then the Lord told Jer-e-mi-ah to take a roll and write the words once more, with more that he would tell him. He told him that when the foe came to take Je-ru-sa-lem, he should be saved.

When Neb-u-chad-nez-zar, king of Bab-y-lon, came to Je-ru-sa-lem, he went in the tem-ple and took all the ves-sels of gold and sil-ver, and he robbed the king's pal-ace. Then he took the king and his peo-ple and all the men fit for war back to Bab-y-lon with him.

Jer-e-mi-ah was thrown in a deep pit full of mire. Zed-

THE PEO-PLE ARE LED OFF AS SLAVES.

e-ki-ah, who had been made king of those left in Je-ru-sa-lem, had him brought to him in se-cret, for he wished to ask him a ques-tion.

Jer-e-mi-ah said, "If I tell thee, wilt thou prom-ise not to put me to death?" The king said he would. He then told the king that he must go out to the king of Bab-y-lon and serve him. But he did not, and soon the Chal-de-ans came and laid siege to the cit-y, and there was no bread to eat.

In the night, Zed-e-ki-ah fled with his two sons, but they caught him, and took him to the king of Bab-y-lon. He killed the sons, and put out Zed-e-ki-ah's eyes, and kept him in chains till he died.

Then the foe burnt the tem-ple, and all the hous-es, and the pal-ace of the king. They broke down the walls, and took off all the gold and sil-ver, and made slaves of the peo-ple. But the king of Bab-y-lon sent word that they must find Jer-e-mi-ah, and be kind to him, and do all that he might ask. The cap-tain told him he might stay in his own land, or go to Bab-y-lon and he would take care of him. But Jer-e-mi-ah stayed in his own land, and more of the Jews came where he lived and stayed with him.

CHAPTER XXX.

THE DRY BONES—THE STO-RY OF DAN-IEL.

Now there was a proph-et named E-ze-ki-el with the men who had been tak-en off by the king of Bab-y-lon. The Lord made him see all the sins that the peo-ple did in Je-ru-sa-lem, how they served false gods and filled the land with sin, and why He meant to pun-ish them. E-ze-ki-el told all to the slaves who were with him, but they would not hear him. But some of them said, "What shall we do? Who can save us?" E-ze-ki-el told them they could be sor-ry for their sins, and turn to the Lord. "Turn ye! turn ye! for why will ye die?"

When the time was up, a man came and told them that all had come to pass as E-ze-ki-el had said. But the Lord said if they would turn to Him, He would bless them. He showed E-ze-ki-el a place full of dry bones, and He made flesh come on them, and skin, and then He breathed on them and made them live. Then He showed him that just so He could raise Is-ra-el out of their low state and bring them to their own land in joy. He said He would make one na-tion of them.

Now the king of Bab-y-lon chose four young men of Is-ra-el to wait on him. They were named Dan-iel, Sha-drach, Me-shach, and A-bed-ne-go.

They were to be taught as the king chose, and he sent them their meals from his own ta-ble. Now the meat and wine sent had been left from that of-fered up to the false gods of the As-syr-i-ans, and the young men would not take it. The chief who had the care of them loved Dan-iel, and he did not want the king to know of this. He said the king would see that they were pale if they did not eat the meat and drink the wine. But Dan-iel begged him to let them eat on-ly pulse for ten days.

He did so, and he saw they were in fine health, with red cheeks. So he did not force them to take the bread and wine. In time they went and served in the king's pal-ace, and pleased him well.

One night the king dreamed a dream that made him sad. He called the wise men and told them that he could not think what it was he had dreamt, and they must find out what it was, and what it meant, or they should be cut to pie-ces.

Then they said, " There was not a man on earth who could do such a thing. It was a strange thing that the king asked—for them to tell his dream when he did not know it him-self. No one but a god could do that, and the gods did not live on the earth."

Then the king said all the wise men should be slain. But Dan-iel asked what the tu-mult meant, and he went to the king and told him that if he gave him time he would find out the dream so that the wise men should not be slain. The king said he would give him time. Dan-iel then asked his three friends to pray to God with him.

Then God showed Dan-iel what the dream was, and what it meant. And Dan-iel said, " I thank thee and praise thee, O God of my fa-thers, that thou hast told me the things the king de-sires to know."

So Dan-i-el was brought in haste to the king. He told him that his God had made known to him what was to come to pass. He said that the king had dreamed that he saw a great im-age, whose head was of gold, but whose feet were clay. As the king saw it, a stone struck it, and it was bro-ken in small pie-ces, so small that the wind blew them a-way. Then the stone grew to a large moun-tain.

This im-age of gold and brass and clay meant all the king-doms of the earth. They must all give way to the king-dom of Christ. The stone meant that king-dom.

Then Neb-u-chad-nez-zar fell on his face and said, " It is

true your God is a God of gods," and he made Dan-iel a great man, and gave him cit-ies to rule, and he gave his three friends good pla-ces too.

Now Neb-u-chad-nez-zar made an i-dol of gold, and sent word to all in the land that they must go and pray to it. Then it was told him that Dan-iel and his friends did not go and pray to the i-dol as he had said.

So the king had them brought to him, and he told them that if they did not o-bey him they should be cast in-to a fi-e-ry fur-nace.

But they did not fear. They said they knew God could save them from death, or if not, they would burn to death be-fore they would serve false gods.

Then the king was in great wrath. He sent word that his men should heat the fur-nace sev-en times hot-ter than it had ev-er been.

Then Dan-iel and his three friends were bound and cast in the flames. The fur-nace was so hot that it killed the men who cast them in; but these three He-brews rose and walked in the fire, for God kept the flames so that it did not e-ven scorch their clothes. Then the king, who looked on, saw four men in the midst of the fire. The form of the fourth was like the Son of God. And the king called out, "Ye serv-ants of the most high God, come forth!" The young men walked out, and their hair was not singed, nor the smell of fire on them.

Then Neb-u-chad-nez-zar blessed the name of their God, and made a law that no one should·speak e-vil of the God of Dan-iel, for there was no oth-er god could save like Him.

Now Bab-y-lon was a grand cit-y, with high walls and ma-ny gates of brass. The king had a fine pal-ace with great gar-dens on a hill, and all men praised him till he thought no more of God. He dreamed once more, and told Dan-iel of it. He dreamed of a green tree, where the birds sang, and beasts lay down in its shade. He thought an an-gel cried out from heav-en, "Cut down the tree, but let the stump stand for sev-en years." The king asked Dan-iel what this meant.

Dan-iel did not like to tell the king at first. But at last he told him, "The tree means thee, O king." And he went on to say that the cut-ting down of the tree, and the stump that was to be left for sev-en years, meant that Neb-u-chad-nez-zar should come down from his throne, and lose his king-dom, and be turned out in the fields with the beasts and have to eat grass like them till he learned that God rules the world, and makes and un-makes kings.

It came to pass that one day, when the king walked in his grand pal-ace, and looked out with pride on all he owned, and said, "Is not this great Bab-y-lon that I have made?" there came a voice from heav-en that told him he must lose it all. And the king lost his mind so that he could not rule, and he knew no more than a dumb beast, and went out and slept on the ground.

But when the time was at an end, Neb-u-chad-nez-zar's sen-ses came back to him, and he prayed to God and praised his name. And God gave his throne back to him, and he served God the rest of his life.

CHAPTER XXXI.

Now when Neb-u-chad-nez-zar was dead, there was a king called Bel-shaz-zar who reigned in Bab-y-lon. He made a great feast, and had the gold and sil-ver ves-sels brought in which had been sto-len from the tem-ple at Je-ru-sa-lem. They drank wine out of these while they praised their false gods.

But all at once they saw a strange sight. There came forth a man's hand that wrote words on the wall. They could not tell what the words meant, but the king was full of fear, and his limbs shook when he saw them. He sent for the wise men, but they could not read them. When the queen heard of it, she said there was a man in the land who could help him, and his name was Dan-iel.

So Dan-iel was sent for, and the king said that if he would tell him what the words on the wall meant, he would give him a scar-let robe, a gold chain, and a high place in the king-dom.

But Dan-iel told him he might keep his gifts. Then he told the king that God meant to say to him in these words that he would have him no long-er for king. "Thy king-dom is at an end, He has tried thee and thou art found want-ing." He has given thy king-dom to the Medes and Per-sians.

Then Bel-shaz-zar did as he had said he would. He made Dan-iel put on a scar-let robe and a gold chain, and he gave him the third rank in his land. But that same night the Medes and Per-sians came, and slew the king, and took the king-dom.

Now it pleased the Per-sian king, Da-ri-us, to put Dan-iel to rule part of the land, and the prin-ces hat-ed him, and sought to find fault in him. But he was so good and wise they could find no thing to say but that he served his God.

Now the king made a law that if a-ny one should ask help from god or man for thir-ty days, they should be cast in a den of li-ons.

The prin-ces were glad, and went and told the king that Dan-iel asked help from his God three times a day.

Now the king loved Dan-iel, but he thought he must stand by his own law. So he told his men to cast him in the den of li-ons, but he said, "Thy God whom thou serv-est, He will save thee."

They took Dan-iel and cast him in the den of li-ons, and rolled a great stone up-on the mouth of the den.

The king was sad and would not eat, and he could not sleep. He rose when it was light, and went to the den, and called Dan-iel to ask if he still lived. Dan-iel said, " My God has sent His an-gel and shut the mouths of the li-ons so they have not hurt me."

The king was glad, and he brought Dan-iel out of the den. Then he had all the men who had spo-ken e-vil of him cast in the den of li-ons with their chil-dren and wives. The li-ons leaped on them and killed them at once. Then King Da-ri-us made a law, and sent it to all parts of the land, that all men must fear and bow down to the God of Dan-iel.

Dan-iel knew that the time would soon come for the Is-ra-el-ites to go back to their own land, and he prayed to God for them, and the Lord sent an an-gel to tell him that the Jews should go back. He told, too, that a Sa-viour would be born and put to death, and then once more the Jews should be driv-en forth.

CHAPTER XXXII.

THE JEWS BUILD UP THE TEM-PLE.

God made Cy-rus, the king at Bab-y-lon, let His peo-ple go. Cy-rus helped them with sil-ver, and gold, and suits of clothes, for God put it in his heart to do so. He gave them back all the ves-sels of gold and sil-ver that had been sto-len from the tem-ple. So they went in a great ar-my to their old home, and found the cit-y of Je-ru-sa-lem in ru-ins, just as it had been left so ma-ny years a-go.

The first thing they did was to build up the al-tar that they might pray to God there. Then they brought wood and stones to build a new tem-ple to the Lord. They were glad, and sent up shouts of joy, but some of the old men wept.

The Sa-mar-i-tans, who lived in the land, came and said, " Let us help you." But the Is-ra-el-ites knew they prayed to i-dols, and they would not let them help. So the Sa-mar-i-tans were an-gry, and did all they could to stop the work. When Cy-rus died, and Ar-tax-erx-es was made king, they wrote to him what the Jews were do-ing. They said if he let the Jews build up their cit-y, they would pay no tax-es to him. If he would ask, he would find out that the Jews in the old time gave much trou-ble.

King Ar-tax-erx-es sent word that they might stop the Jews in build-ing the tem-ple. So the Jews went to work

BUILD-ING A NEW TEM-PLE.

and built fine hous-es to live in, and when there was a new king of Per-sia they did not try to find out if he would let them build the tem-ple. Then the Lord was not pleased with them, but sent word by Hag-ga-i that if they did not build His tem-ple at once He would not bless or help them.

The Sa-mar-i-tans tried to stop them once more, but King Da-ri-us sent word to them to leave the Jews in peace. He made a law, too, that the Sa-mar-i-tans should pay a tax to the Jews to help them in their work.

There was a good priest in Bab-y-lon named Ez-ra. He was a Jew, and he longed to go to his own peo-ple. He asked leave of the king to go, and God made the king so kind that he gave him rich gifts to take with him. The Jews who chose to do so went with him.

He was in great grief when he heard that some of the prin-ces at Je-ru-sa-lem had wives who prayed to false gods.

He wept and prayed to God for these men, and they came to him and said they would give up these wives, who might lead them to sin and leave the true God.

CHAPTER XXXIII.

THE STO-RY OF ES-THER.

THERE were still some of the Jews in the land of Per-sia when A-has-u-e-rus was made king. He held a great feast in his fine pal-ace of Shu-shan, and the men drank wine out of ves-sels of sil-ver and gold. On the sev-enth day he sent for Vash-ti, his queen, to show her to the prin-ces, for she was fair to look up-on.

But Vash-ti would not go, and the king was an-gry. One of the wise men said no wo-man in Per-sia would o-bey her hus-band when she heard what the queen had done. Then they told the king that he ought to make a law that Vash-ti should come no more to the king, and he must choose a new queen. So should each man rule in his own house.

The king did as the wise man said. He sent word to all parts of his land that the fair-est of the young girls should be sent for him to choose from. Now there was in the pal-ace a Jew named Mor-de-cai who had a fair young cous-in called Es-ther. It came to pass that Es-ther was brought with the rest of the girls, but no one knew she was a Jew-ess.

When King A-has-u-e-rus saw Es-ther, he loved her more than the rest, and he put the crown on her head, and made her queen. Then he made a feast for her, and gave gifts to all in the house.

Not long aft-er this Mor-de-cai found out a plot to kill the king, and he made it known to Es-ther so that the men were hung.

Now there was a man named Ha-man in the king's house who hated Mor-de-cai. He was a great man, and all bowed down to him but this Jew, and he made up his mind that he would make an end of him, and of all the Jews in the land. So he spoke to the king a-gainst the

Jews.   He told him they had their own laws, and did not
keep the king's laws.   He said that if the king would
make a law to kill all the Jews, he would pay him ten
thou-sand tal-ents of sil-ver.

The king heard him, and took a ring from his fin-ger
and gave it to Ha-man.   He meant that Ha-man might
write what he chose and seal it with that ring.

So Ha-man was glad, and wrote out a law that on a
cer-tain day ev-er-y Jew, man, wo-man or child, in Per-sia
should be killed.   And the one who killed a Jew could
take his house and lands and all he had for his own.
Then he sent forth word of this law through all the land
by means of let-ters sealed with the king's ring.

When Mor-de-cai heard of this he rent his clothes, and
put on sack-cloth, and went out in the streets to the king's
gates and mourned there.   And in all the land the Jews
wept and cried.

Now Queen Es-ther had not heard of the law, but some
one told her that Mor-de-cai was in sack-cloth, and that
he cried in the streets.   Es-ther was grieved, and sent to
ask what was the mat-ter.   Mor-de-cai told the man of
Ha-man's wick-ed plot, and said that the queen ought to
go to the king and beg for the lives of her peo-ple.

Then the queen sent word that no one dared to go to
the king whom he did not send for.   If one went, and the
king did not hold out his gold-en scep-tre, that one would
be put to death.   And she said the king had not sent for
her for thir-ty days.

The man went and told Mor-de-cai.   He sent word to

the queen, " Do not think be-cause thou art queen that thou wilt be spared when all the Jews are killed. Who can tell but thou hast been made queen so as to save them."

Then Es-ther sent word to Mor-de-cai that he must tell all the Jews to fast three days. She said she would fast too with her maid-ens, and then she would go to the king, and " If I die, I must die."

So the third day Es-ther put on her rich robes, and went in and stood where the king could see her. God made him feel kind to her, and he held out his gold-en scep-tre and asked what was her wish. He said he would give it to her if it were the half of his king-dom.

Then Es-ther asked the king to come with Ha-man to a feast at her house that day and he said they would come. Now the king knew that Es-ther had some fa-vor to ask, but she did not ask it that day. She begged the king to come to a feast on the next day. Ha-man's heart was proud that he should be asked once more by the queen. But still he could not be hap-py for Mor-de-cai did not bow to him in the gate. He told his wife how it galled him, and she said he must build a tall gal-lows, and beg the king to have Mor-de-cai hung on it. Then he could go and feast with the queen with a glad heart.

That night the king could not sleep. He made his serv-ant bring the book in which was set down all that had hap-pened in his reign. The man read it to him, and then it told how Mor-de-cai had once saved the king's life.

Then the king asked what had been done for Mor-de-cai, and the man said noth-ing had been done. Just then

Ha-man came in. He meant to ask the king to have Mor-de-cai hung on the gal-lows he had built.

·The king asked him at once, "What shall be done for a man the king wants to hon-or?"

Ha-man thought, "The king means me." So he said, "Let the king's robes and his crown be brought to him, and let him put them on, and let him ride on the king's horse, and let a prince lead it through the streets and cry, 'Thus shall it be done to the man whom the king de-lights to hon-or!'"

Then the king said, "Make haste, and take the crown and robes, and the horse, and do to Mor-de-cai, the Jew, as thou hast said."

Ha-man did not dare say no to the king, so he took the king's robes and crown to Mor-de-cai, and set him on the king's horse, and led him through the streets as he had said. Then he went to his home in shame and rage.

But he had to go to the feast of the queen that day with the king. When the king asked Es-ther once more what was her wish she spoke out, "Let the king save my life, and the lives of all my peo-ple, the Jews. For e-vil things have been told the king that are not true, and we have been sold to be slain."

Then the king asked, "Who is the man that dared to do these things?" and the queen said, "Ha-man."

Ha-man fell down and begged for his life, but some one told the king that there was a tall gal-lows near, which Ha-man had built for Mor-de-cai. Then the king said, "Hang him on it;" and it was done.

THE KING BIDS THAT HA-MAN BE HUNG.

Then the king gave Es-ther Ha-man's house, and he sent for Mor-de-cai, and took off his ring and gave it to him, and he let him make a new law and seal it with the ring. This new let-ter said that the Jews had leave to slay all that came to harm them. So it came to pass that God made them strong on that day, and their foes fled from them. Then the Jews were full of joy, and kept a feast each year at that time.

CHAPTER XXXIV.

There was a man in the land of Uz named Job. He was a just and good man, and God had made him rich and great. He had sev-en sons and three daugh-ters.

But the Lord sent tri-als to Job, to see if he would still love and serve him. He lost his rich-es and his chil-dren. One day a man came and told that rob-bers had sto-len his cat-tle, and killed his serv-ants. Then one told of fire from the sky that had burnt his sheep and those who took care of them. Then men stole his cam-els.

But more sad than all, he heard that while his chil-dren feast-ed at one house, a great wind came and blew down the house so that all were killed.

Job rent his clothes, and bowed down to the earth, and said, "I brought noth-ing in-to the world, and I shall take noth-ing out. The Lord gave, and the Lord has tak-en a-way; bless-ed be the name of the Lord." So Job did not sin or speak e-vil of God.

Then God tried Job with a sore sick-ness. Boils came on him from his head to his feet. His wife came to him and said, "Curse God and die."

But Job told her she was sin-ful. He said, "Shall we take good things from the hand of the Lord, and shall we not take e-vil things?"

Now Job had three friends who came to see him.

They rent their clothes and wept when they saw him, he was so changed. At first they could not speak. They thought all his tri-als had been sent for his sins. They said at last, "If thou hast sinned, do so no more, and God will for-give and make thee well."

Job knew he had done no wrong, so he said, "Let me a-lone. I did not send for you, and you do not com-fort me at all. The Lord hath sent great tri-als on me; I would rath-er die than live. Yet I know that my Sa-viour liv-eth, and I shall rise up from my grave, and see God."

ILL NEWS IS BROUGHT TO JOB.

But the three friends kept on with their talk, as though he must have sinned, and that all his tri-als were sent for his sins. Job grew an-gry with them.

Then a voice came to them out of a whirl-wind, and it was the voice of God. It spoke of all God's works, and asked if Job could do the least of them.

Job bowed down to the earth, and asked God to for-give all his sins, and he prayed for the three friends too.

Then the Lord healed Job, and blessed him, and made him twice as rich, and gave him more sons and daugh-ters, and he lived to be a ver-y old man.

CHAPTER XXXV.

THE STO-RY OF JO-NAH.

THERE was a great and wick-ed cit-y called Nin-e-veh in those days. It was full of grand hous-es, and gar-dens, and pal-a-ces. The walls were so wide that three char-i-ots could drive side by side on them, and had tow-ers where the guard could stand and shoot down ar-rows on their foes.

Now God spoke to Jo-nah, and told him to go to Nin-e-veh and preach to the peo-ple of their sins. Jo-nah feared to go, and tried to hide from the Lord.

He went on a ship at Jop-pa, but God sent a great storm and the crew were a-fraid. They prayed to their false gods, and threw out some of the car-go of the ship, so that it would not sink. Jo-nah was fast a-sleep, but they woke him and begged him to call on his God for help.

The men said there must be some one in the ship who had done some great sin, and they cast lots to find out who it might be.

The lot fell on Jo-nah, and they said, "Tell us what sin thou hast done? Where art thou from?"

And Jo-nah told them why he was there. Then they said, "What shall we do?"

Jo-nah said, "Cast me in the sea and it will be still, for it is for my sin the storm is sent."

Then the men rowed hard and tried to bring the ship to land, but they could not. Then they prayed to Jo-nah's God that He would not count it sin for them if they cast him in the sea.

So they took him and cast him in the sea, and it grew calm at once. From that time those men served the Lord.

There was a great fish sent to swal-low Jo-nah, and he was in that fish three days and nights. Then he prayed to God, and was sor-ry for his sin, and God heard him, and made the fish cast him out on dry land.

Then the Lord told him once more to go to Nin-e-veh, and say to all what He had told him. So Jo-nah went and cried out in a loud voice, "Aft-er for-ty days Nin-e-veh shall fall for the sins of her peo-ple."

When the king of Nin-e-veh heard this, he thought that it was true, and that the Lord had sent Jo-nah. He left his throne and took off his rich robes and put on sack-cloth. And he sent word to all his peo-ple that they must fast and pray. They must not eat, or drink, or wear fine clothes, but each one must put on sack-cloth, and ask

God to for-give his sins. When God heard their pray-ers, He pit-ied them, and did not de-stroy the cit-y.

Now Jo-nah was not pleased at this. He want-ed all these peo-ple killed be-cause he had preached that they would be. He thought they would laugh at him and call him a false proph-et. So he said to the Lord, " I knew thou wouldst not de-stroy the cit-y when I fled the first time. And now, O Lord, put me to death, for I would rath-er die than live."

A VINE GROWS TO SHIELD JO-NAH FROM THE SUN.

The Lord was still kind to Jo-nah. When he went out from Nin-e-veh and stopped near the cit-y, the Lord made a vine to grow up in one night and shield him from the hot sun. The next night a worm gnawed the root so the vine died. Then once more he was not pleased and wished to die, for the sun beat on him and made him faint.

Then God said, "Thou art an-gry that I killed the gourd that grew up in a night and died in a night, yet thou wouldst have me de-stroy Nin-e-veh, that great cit-y in which are ma-ny thou-sand lit-tle chil-dren so young they can not tell their right hands from their left."

So the Lord showed Jo-nah how much in the wrong he had been to find fault with the ways of God.

CHAPTER XXXVI.

NE-HE-MI-AH.

In the days when Ar-tax-erx-es was king of Per-sia, there was a Jew named Ne-he-mi-ah who served him with wine. Some men came to the court one day who told him of the state of ru-in that Je-ru-sa-lem was in, with its walls down, and the gates ly-ing on the ground.

Ne-he-mi-ah wept at the thought of this. The king saw how sad he looked when he gave him the cup of wine, and he asked him the cause of his grief. When Ne-he-mi-ah told him, the king said, "What dost thou ask of me?"

Ne-he-mi-ah prayed to God in his heart that He would make the king grant his wish, and then he said, "I pray thee send me to Je-ru-sa-lem that I may build up its walls."

The Lord made the king let Ne-he-mi-ah go, and he sent a guard with him, and let-ters to the head men through the land to help him.

Now there were two of the head men, San-bal-lat and To-bi-ah, who did not like what the king had done, and when Ne-he-mi-ah had set the Jews to work to build up the walls, they laid a plot to come and kill them while they worked. But the Jews heard of this, and while half of them worked, the oth-ers kept watch, and e-ven those who worked had their swords and shields near them.

Soon the walls were built so far that the foes feared to come to Je-ru-sa-lem. Then they sent word that it was said Ne-he-mi-ah meant to be king of the Jews, and that the king of Per-sia should hear of it if Ne-he-mi-ah did not come and talk to them. They meant to kill him if he came to them, but Ne-he-mi-ah would not go.

At last the walls and gates were built, and the peo-ple gave them to the Lord to be His for all time, and they made a feast with great joy.

Ne-he-mi-ah went to Per-sia for a while, and when he came back from there he found that the peo-ple had not kept their vows to the Lord. They had made friends with the hea-then and had tak-en wives from them. They had not brought a tenth of their grain and fruits to the Le-vites, so that the Le-vites had to give up the works of the tem-ple that they might raise grain for food.

Ne-he-mi-ah was grieved, and he called the priests and Le-vites back to the tem-ple. He saw men at work on the Sab-bath day, and he told them that God had pun-ished the Jews of old for such sins. He said the gates of the cit-y must be shut till the Sab-bath was o-ver.